ADVANCE PRAISE FOR *The Goat Fish and the Lover's Knot*

"You'll savor every word as Driscoll sings the sad, sweet songs of rural America. These songs believe in heartaches and miracles. These miracles look up at the stars and see humanity in the constellations."
BONNIE JO CAMPBELL | author of *Mothers, Tell Your Daughters*

"A new book by Jack Driscoll is a cause for celebration. *The Goat Fish and the Lover's Knot* reminds me—not that I'd forgotten—exactly why Driscoll has long been one of my favorite American writers. The qualities that have made his work indelible—his deeply intimate relationship with the natural world, the natural lyricism, and palpability of his language, the authentic way in which his always credible narratives earn their mystery—are here in abundance in this beautiful collection."
STUART DYBEK | author of *The Start of Something: The Selected Stories of Stuart Dybek*

"These are tales of family mayhem and magic—of how love survives and how we survive love—each of them told in the rich, wry voice of the real. Jack Driscoll is a local hero to Michigan writers; this book proves him a national treasure."
PETER HO DAVIES | author of *The Fortunes*

"In this new collection, Jack Driscoll has proven himself again to be one of the finest fiction writers at work these days. His great gift is how uniquely he is able to bestow complexity upon his characters, complete their humanity with just this or that perfect detail, or gesture, or line of dialogue. Combined with the empathy that, as a writer, he shows for all of them, along with his sly eye for foibles and absurdities, reading his fiction feels like living it, and you come away from his pages under his influence, with a deeper vision of your own, feeling understood and better able to understand. There's no sentimentality

in *The Goat Fish and the Lover's Knot*, but Driscoll is able to see through others' eyes in a way few writers can, and his work adds to the world's store of compassion. And, such language! Without ever compromising the power and immediacy and pull of his stories, his sentences often just have to be reread and admired. There's everything in this book that a work of fiction can give us—suspense, and comfort, and conflict, and character, and poetry, and landscape, and sanity, and craziness. It's the kind of book that renews one's belief in the power and importance of books."

LAURA KASISCHKE | author of *The Infinitesimals*

"Every sentence written by Jack Driscoll is a miracle—and every story bright with humor and heart and insight. *The Goat Fish and the Lover's Knot* will hypnotize you with its lyrical beauty."

BENJAMIN PERCY | author of *Thrill Me, The Dead Lands, Red Moon, The Wilding,* and *Refresh, Refresh*

THE
GOAT FISH
AND THE
LOVER'S KNOT

MADE IN MICHIGAN WRITERS SERIES

General Editors

Michael Delp,
Interlochen Center for the Arts

M. L. Liebler,
Wayne State University

Advisory Editors

Melba Joyce Boyd
Wayne State University

Stuart Dybek
Western Michigan University

Kathleen Glynn

Jerry Herron
Wayne State University

Laura Kasischke
University of Michigan

Thomas Lynch

Frank Rashid
Marygrove College

Doug Stanton

Keith Taylor
University of Michigan

A complete listing of the books in this series can be found online at wsupress.wayne.edu

STORIES BY JACK DRISCOLL

THE
GOAT FISH
AND THE
LOVER'S KNOT

Wayne State University Press
Detroit

ISBN 978-0-8143-4295-4 (paperback)
ISBN 978-0-8143-4296-1 (e-book)

Library of Congress Control Number: 2016959425

∞

Wayne State University Press
Leonard N. Simons Building
4809 Woodward Avenue
Detroit, Michigan 48201-1309

Visit us online at wsupress.wayne.edu

Publication of this book was made possible by a generous gift from The Meijer Foundation. Additional support provided by the Michigan Council for Arts and Cultural Affairs and the National Endowment for the Arts.

For Barry Lopez

Here I sat on a boulder by the winter-steaming river and put my
head in my hands and considered time—which is next to
nothing, merely what vanishes, and yet can make one's elbows
nearly pierce one's thighs.

GALWAY KINNELL

CONTENTS

Acknowledgments ix

The Goat Fish and the Lover's Knot 1

All The Time in the World 15

Calcheck and Priest 31

The Alchemist's Apprentice 53

Land of the Lost and Found 71

The Good Father 87

A Woman Gone Missing 99

Here's How It Works 115

On This Day You Are All Your Ages 131

That Story 147

ACKNOWLEDGMENTS

These stories, some in slightly different forms, appeared in the following publications:

"The Good Father" in *Agni Online*; "The Goat Fish and the Lover's Knot," "All the Time in the World," "A Woman Gone Missing," "That Story," and "On This Day You Are All Your Ages" in *The Georgia Review*; "Calcheck and Priest" in *Michigan Quarterly Review*; "The Alchemist's Apprentice" and "Land of the Lost and Found" in *Prairie Schooner*.

"That Story" was reprinted in the 2012 *Pushcart Prize Anthology*.

"All the Time in the World" was reprinted in the 2015 *New Stories from the Midwest*.

My heartfelt thanks to the National Endowment for the Arts for a Creative Writing Fellowship that supported the completion of this story collection.

To Stephen Corey for his support and eagle eye over three decades, and to the editors of all the journals in which these stories first appeared.

THE GOAT FISH AND THE LOVER'S KNOT

I TOLD MY DAD, "As far as I know," when he asked if the entire clan would be there. Meaning my best friend Darwin and both his parents, Mr. and Mrs. LaVann, who owned a cabin on a lake about an hour's drive north of Cadillac in decent weather. And, although we couldn't have known it then, that was where the sheriff's department deputies would search first thing after Mrs. LaVann went missing. "Went renegade" was how Darwin would amend it after she finally did call from somewhere far out of state, but only to let them know that she was alive and not to worry and that she'd come back home when she could. When she was ready. Though of course she never did.

She was secretive and distant and had a foreign sounding name, which was how, a year earlier, she'd introduced herself to me the first time I stopped at their house after school: Marenza Czarny. I imagined some war-torn country, like maybe she'd been a refugee or something, but when I later asked Darwin where she was originally from, he said, "Bay City. Born and raised." She'd *dreamed* the name and legally changed hers *to* it the day she turned eighteen. "A conversion," he said and rolled his eyes, but he offered up no details, and I left it at that.

My dad would not have liked her: Tall and thin, high cheekbones and long, shiny-dark hair with red highlights that showed through in the sun. Not a line in her face. The kind of beauty that rarely—if ever—was available to men such as my dad, men who knew it and so maligned its very existence.

I calculated her to be mid-thirties, max, a good ten years younger than her husband. Together they constituted the most perplexing mismatch I'd ever seen. Not that Mr. LaVann wasn't upbeat and good-natured enough. And occasionally he was even fun to be around, and way less strict than most other dads. But he had one of those fat, flat faces, like he might have played tuba in junior high band. How he and his wife had gotten together defied in my imagination what a certain woman's attraction to a man might be. Other than money. He'd spend his afternoons drinking coffee and poring over spreadsheets fanned out across their dining room table.

DARWIN AND I HAD BOTH turned fourteen that summer our lives changed, and then changed back, though possibly not for the better.

Anyway, it was Mrs. LaVann—that's what I called her to be polite, and she never corrected me—who said at the lake one day, "Here," and handed us half a dozen perfectly good pie tins. "See if you boys can find a suitable use for these."

True, I'd yet to see her bake anything. Or cook for that matter, unless sliding a bagel into the toaster oven qualified. We bypassed panning for gold, and Darwin grabbed a hammer instead, punching a hole through each tin with a single swing and a ten-penny nail. Then we hung them from a gnarly apple tree branch with different lengths of fifteen-pound monofilament: giant wind chimes that we took aim at and made dance and spin with at least a thousand high-pitched BB dings.

Their cabin was rustic, "weather distressed" as Mr. LaVann put it. Authentic. "It's a look people pay for," he said and shrugged, and I wondered if that held true for the slightly cockeyed windows and the skull plate and antlers anchored above the front door. There were exposed beams and a shallow-pitched corrugated metal roof that sounded, whenever it rained, like snare drums. "Vintage 1950s," he said. "Someone's change-jar, one-board-at-a-time dream getaway." One that he'd picked up for a song, he said.

When I later mentioned this to my dad, like maybe we could swing it, too, *our* own vacation place, he just nodded, the canned laugh track from some TV sitcom filling up our living room, my mom silently clapping her hands. "Pandering *shit*coms," as my dad called them, came as close as my mom, withdrawn and prone to depression, was apt to get to making it through each day.

It can happen—it *does* happen—the doctors concurred, with a bad enough scare. That scare turned out to be having kids—having me.

She never offered advice one way or another on much of anything. Mostly she'd go silent and look away. It was my dad who tagged on me to canvas the neighborhood. "Go door to door," he said, "and lock in a few contracts weeding and edging and mowing lawns. A paper route—it's not too late. Hell's bells, sell some damn crickets and night crawlers to the local bait shops if that's what it takes. Anything to get you centered. To do right by what's expected of you around here."

I didn't really know what that was. Better grades, a tidier bedroom. Community college looming somewhere in my future? Or possibly enlistment in the army, which would at least lock on to one thing we'd have in common. He'd spent two tours in Vietnam, just before the war ended.

"That's the problem with your generation," he said. "With all you kids. Everyone's lost and mouthy and muddle-minded. Can't think straight or tell fake from real, the goddamn Hope Diamond from a glass doorknob up the ass."

He said something about pursuit—what he called "pressing ahead, no matter what"—as opposed to selfishness and extravagance and greed. Suckering up to the almighty dollar. This was epitomized, though he didn't name names, by Mr. LaVann, his money clip, and his Oldsmobile '88 convertible with a front seat so deep and soft it was more like driving a couch.

I'd never openly contradict anything my dad said. But sometimes, to secretly get back at him, I'd sit on *our* couch and imagine a steering wheel and a tinted windshield, and then fantasize about running the back roads after I got my driver's license in another couple of years. Top down and the radio blasting and, hopefully by then, a girlfriend crowding right up tight to my shoulder and hip, throwing her arm around me.

By contrast my dad pointed out that he'd never in his entire life owned a new car, a fancy redesigned model straight off the showroom floor. He bought used and hadn't missed a day of work in twenty years. "And why do you suppose we buy butter and cheese by the brick?" he'd ask. "Any idea, Wayne? Any clue whatsoever?"

He sold life insurance, his sales pitch being that if the dead could speak, who would they thank? "That is correct . . . yours truly," he'd say. "All those grieving wives and daughters and sons of the deceased."

Mr. LaVann, on the other hand, had made a killing manufacturing deep fryers, a business he'd started, and which now afforded him as much time off as he wanted—weeks and weeks. Like Darwin and me, he had the entire summer to just screw around and be a kid again. Raise some innocent hell, he said, that you could later translate into stories to joke and laugh about. He claimed Dunkin' Donuts and Burger King as clients, but I'd never once gotten any freebies when I'd bike over to either establishment and drop his name, as if *I* were his heir and only living son.

At his angriest, my dad actually had trembling hands when he talked to me, his face turning crimson, as if the very air I breathed was bankrupting our household.

"Okay?" he'd say, pointing close up as if he meant to poke my chest, and I'd nod and nod like, yes, I understand. "Do you?" he'd say, like deep down he knew that such a narrow, insistent certainty such as his could never dictate where I was headed in my life. I hated how every conversation took on the urgency of a hurricane or tornado drill, and all I really wanted was to get as far away from the dangers of that house as quickly as I could. So when the LaVanns invited me—their treat, they said—to spend an entire month with them, I jumped at the chance. Against all odds I appealed to my mom—who, for once, when the subject came up that night at dinner, turned to my dad and said, "Harold. It's too late. I've already told him he can."

THE CABIN had only two bedrooms, so I slept alone on a cot in the loft. Back then I was not a sound sleeper. Almost any noise and I'd be wide-awake, listening, as I was that night, already halfway through my stay, to those same low-grade whimpers and moans, which I anticipated but still hadn't grown accustomed to.

Why I opened my eyes and stared out at the lake, its shimmery pewter-colored surface, I'm not sure. Maybe to concentrate my attention away from what was going on right below me. It never lasted very long, and afterward the cabin always quieted, and eventually I'd doze off. But when I heard footsteps, and then the screen door slowly opening and closing with a slight wheeze of the hinges, Mrs. LaVann appeared on the lawn: not ghostlike, exactly, though the moon was bright, and ground mist lifted and resettled in thin, vaporous clouds around her.

I had no trouble seeing that she was naked, and how she took hold of the hand pump's heavy red arm. She lifted and depressed it three or four times until the water gurgled and then surged full force. On a rope around her neck hung a bar of soap that glistened white as snow and no doubt felt just as cold when she spread her legs and washed herself down there, and then rinsed off, which seemed, even for her, an odd and unusual way to shower, given that there was always plenty of hot water inside.

I wondered if she was okay. If maybe she was feverish or tipsy or possibly sleepwalking. She did not look up to where I was spying down on her, if that's what it constituted, and by the time I got outside she'd already wrapped a towel around herself, and she didn't appear all that startled or surprised to see me.

I pretended I hadn't known that she was out there. I said, "Oh, sorry. I was just about to head out fishing," which on a lot of nights would have been true. With one hand she held on to the spot where she'd tucked in the towel flap below her breastbone, and she smiled and—as if I'd asked—said, "I just needed a little fresh air is all."

I nodded as though I understood, and she nodded, too, as if standing there together was the most ordinary occurrence in the world. A complete nonevent like almost everything else that summer, meaning that we could pretty much come and go as we pleased—me and Darwin, together or alone—and so I'd tiptoe out with my spinning rod and tackle box and row to the north end of the lake, into a certain cove of stumps and sunken deadfall where the fishing was always way better. Walleyes, mostly, which I'd catch with glow-in-the-dark split-tail jigs, and when I'd get back I'd tie the stringer to a dock cleat and wait until first light to gut and clean them. Usually everyone else slept in, and like magic there'd be a batch of fresh fillets in the refrigerator, the flesh as orange as spawning steelhead or salmon. Sometimes I'd leave a fish whole if it was big enough, head and all, and Mr. LaVann would stuff it with breadcrumbs, olive oil, and garlic, and then wrap it in tinfoil and grill it for dinner. And, as if it were part of a ritual, he'd salute me and wink.

ONE MORNING a week or so before the pump incident, Mrs. LaVann, always the earliest riser after me, pushed her chair back a little ways from the table and slung one long leg over the other when I entered the kitchen from outside. She was barefoot and wearing a sleeveless, loose-fitting cotton sundress, the neckline not so low, but plenty low enough. I'd recently undergone a growth spurt, and, at almost 5' 8", just looking down to meet her eyes made me nervous enough. "Are you having a decent time here, Wayne?" she said.

"Yes. Thank you. I like there not being any neighbors, and that this time we're not just up for the weekend." I said, "And I like hearing the loons, too," and mentioned that even though my dad rarely took me, fishing was my number-one favorite thing to do.

"Come over here," she said, and I did. "Now give me your hand." And with her polished red thumbnail she carefully lifted maybe half a dozen scales from my palm that I had no idea were there.

I liked how that felt kind of tickly, and I said, "Yeah, I was out again last night."

"Yes, I know. All by yourself on the water. I wonder, what would your parents say about that? "

"I'd never tell them, uh-uh. And Darwin, he's sworn to secrecy. He'd never say otherwise, and in return I don't bug *him* to go with me. He gets antsy if the action's slow, and he hates changing baits. He says we ought to chum them with a few blasting caps. Every closed-mouthed lunker down there would turn belly-up, and all we'd need is a long-handled net to heft them into the boat."

"He takes after his dad in a lot of ways," she said. "He'll do well in a man's world." She smiled at that, and when she let go of my hand I took a few tentative reverse steps and stopped.

"I'm always careful, Mrs. LaVann. And I'm a strong swimmer." And then right out of nowhere, she said something about train miles. Like they were somehow calculated differently, and that there was a whole other universe out there, which she believed, over time, I'd see my share of. "I hope you do. It's in you," she said, and I thanked her for that, too.

That was as close as we'd come to a quiet, private conversation, prior to finding myself with her as she stood nude behind a quarter inch of towel. And her saying, "Maybe one of these times you'll take me with you. I don't fish, but I could swim close behind in your wake. I'd like that. Something to break the monotony. Something different to look forward to."

I said, "Sure. If I see you out here," and I imagined muscling the oars in a way I'd never done before, and how I'd help her into the boat if she got chilled or exhausted, or if she simply felt like shooting the breeze on a laid-back midnight boat ride.

IT WASN'T A LAKE that accommodated pleasure crafts, pontoons, or ski boats. Or even those low-horsepower outboard putt-putts you sometimes saw on johnboats or on the flat backs of canoes on other lakes. As Mr. LaVann pointed out, there was not a single public launch site anywhere. And the cedar shoreline was so dense and tangled and spongy that if you somehow shimmied through and took half a dozen steps in any direction you might never, even with a compass, find your way back. Thousands and thousands of wilderness acres were forever decomposing along the water's edge, so when the air got muggy some afternoons and lightning struck high up in the sky, a bitter taste of sulfur intensified tenfold on your tongue.

Darwin and I explored only as far as we could pole into the inlets and feeder creeks, which were crystal clear and shallow, and where one time we found the bone-white spine and ribcage of what had to be a black bear.

"Or some fucking Sasquatch," Darwin said, and we reversed as fast as we could to get out of there and back into the lake. "Come on, let's just haul ass out of here," he said, but I was sweaty and hot and mosquito bitten, and so I stripped to my Jockeys. And when I dove in I stroked hard for the silty bottom, where there were water pockets so frigid you could feel, in a matter of seconds, your lips turning purple and your nuts contracting to the size of twin pearls.

I stayed under for as long as I could, close to a full minute and a half, and when I surfaced Darwin was just sitting there motionless and smoking a cigarette. Each day he'd pilfer a few from his mom as she floated on her back out front of the cabin. I wasn't sure if Mr. LaVann even owned a swimsuit, and ankle-deep was as far into the lake as I'd seen him wade—his pants rolled up, his shin bones pale and hairless—to yell to his wife that he was headed into town. That he had a shopping list, and errands to run, and was there anything else that she needed? "Hey, do you hear me? I'm talking to you."

One time he actually broke open a roll of quarters and skimmed maybe two or three bucks' worth, one after the other, across the calm, flat surface right at her before he turned and walked away. I imagined her wincing, as I'd seen her do on occasion when she heard him pull off the two-track and into their driveway. She didn't quilt, or play solitaire, or read paperback novels, and so I figured maybe *this* was her hobby: drowning out her husband's voice, her head tilted back and her ears submerged. But maybe whatever understanding they'd reached as a couple might be solid enough to survive these momentary standoffs.

"How does she stay in so long?" I once asked Darwin. She was way thin, her one-piece tight and shiny black like sealskin, and he said, straight-faced and matter-of-factly, "She's part reptile."

"Right," I said. "And the sun's her heat lamp." He just stared at me like, *Wait long enough and you'll find out.*

And that's exactly what I did, with only one week left before I'd have to go back home, and two weeks before I'd have to go back to school and Ms. Cosgrove's English class. She was one of those teachers who believed that not only would we smarten up by incorporating into our limited vocabularies the Word of the Day, but that we'd become more worldly for it. I'd managed just fine thus far, without any heavy-duty studying, to maintain a straight B average. I hated school, so above all else I did not want the summer to end. I even considered, as a protest, sneaking into the classroom early on the very first day and erasing whatever exotic, impossible-to-remember word she'd written on the blackboard and substituting DAREDEVIL, or JITTERBUG, or HULA POPPER.

I'd been thinking a lot about Mrs. LaVann, how she'd do this lotus thing out on the far end of the dock. Just hunker motionless out there for an hour or more, nothing moving, her arms held out like she might rise and silently fly away without ever once looking back.

It was strange sometimes to think of her as Darwin's mom. Or anyone's mom. As foolish and misguided as I might have been, I'd wait for her outside in the boat for up to half an hour before I'd give up and push off on my own. Not to fish, which in itself should have been a sign, but rather to lie back on those two life preservers that neither

Darwin nor I ever wore. Not even that time an early evening thunderstorm blew up out of nowhere, and he, on his knees, grabbed hold of the gunnels while I navigated the wind-driven swells until we beached just a few feet from where his mom was standing, soaked to the bone and sipping a glass of wine, her sunglasses pushed back on her head.

"Good thing your father wasn't here to witness that," she said, and I noticed the corked bottle in the sand by her feet. She always drank more in her husband's absence, and he'd been away this time for three straight days and nights. I wondered if Darwin had ever asked to go home with him, if I'd be given the choice to stay, which is what I would have done. Then maybe I'd lie to Mrs. LaVann about how, for special occasions, like Thanksgiving or Christmas at our house, I'd get to sip some wine, though in truth I'd yet to experience the effects of even a single drop. And, until that summer at the lake, the urge hadn't culminated in anything more than an invitation from Joanna Pliss, a girl I liked okay, to someday steal a couple of my dad's Miller Lites, and then together we'd figure out the right time and place—which we never did.

It wasn't until the night before we were supposed to leave that Mrs. LaVann materialized out of nowhere. I don't think I ever really believed—just hoped—she would show up to swim behind me, but when I bent to untie the bowline and stood back up, I found her there. The water was warmer than the air, but still I'd put on a sweatshirt and long pants and a Tigers baseball cap. But there *she* was wearing a bikini, one I hadn't seen before. My eyes had already adjusted to the dark, but the bright yellow iridescence half-blinded me like a flashbulb.

She leaned toward me and whispered, "All set?" and before I could even answer she stepped to the edge of the dock and shallow-dove, and when she surfaced she was already stroking toward the middle of the lake.

Have I mentioned the lake's name? It's Half Moon. Or that my mom is 5' 2" and overweight and afraid most days to leave the house? That my dad is my dad, but everything in this life is conditional, like it or not? He wouldn't have liked me standing upright late at night in a tippy fourteen-foot aluminum rowboat so I could keep a watch on my best friend's mom. I fastened on her and did not for one second look away. Not up or sideways, and especially not back toward the cabin where a light, at any moment, might come on.

For a few seconds I *would* lose her, but each time she'd reappear when the clouds separated and those star clusters cast just enough illumination for me to spot her yellow backside, like a trapline buoy being towed by some monster pike or muskie.

I'd taken one oar out of its lock to use like a paddle, wishing that Mr. LaVann had equipped the boat with one of those high-intensity sealed-beam searchlights powerful enough to cut through mist or fog, reaching out a hundred feet or more.

"Slow down," I wanted to call out, but even soft talking carried across the water, and the last thing I needed was for Darwin or his dad to hear me and discover the two of us missing. The plan, or so I *thought*, was for Mrs. LaVann to breaststroke directly behind the boat as I rowed. A slow, relaxed pace. I wondered if she had any idea where she was, or where she was headed, like possibly to some sunken island I hadn't discovered, where suddenly, from out of the deep heart of the lake, there she'd be, standing up to her knees and waving me in, the other hand planted on her hip.

That, however, did not, and still doesn't, approximate what transpired. Had things gone differently, gone badly, and had I been called to testify, I would have sworn to nothing more than a summer about to end, a final boat ride, and a woman I suspected had already entered the final days of her marriage and who, for some reason, wanted me to know that.

But no one would ever ask. No one would be up waiting for us, to hear how my chest had tightened and how, fearing the worst *and* having lapsed into panic, I'd cupped my hands around my mouth as I'd quietly called her name. I don't remember how many times. Over and over, and in every possible direction. "Answer me, please. Answer me wherever you are."

When finally she did, she said, "Wayne, I'm right here." Exactly where she was supposed to be, just a few feet behind the boat, which sat in a still drift while she treaded water right there below me.

I said, "Jesus, Mrs. LaVann," though I was hyperventilating so badly I almost couldn't get the words out, and my teeth were chattering. "I thought you'd drowned."

"No, no," she said. "I'm sorry. I was on my back, just thinking about things. You've seen me do that every day. And how distant and muted the world becomes underwater. And besides, I'm a floater. I couldn't sink if I wanted to. I'd have to jump overboard hugging an anchor."

"I couldn't see you anywhere," I said. "And nothing else mattered. It didn't make sense something so awful could happen."

"Here, help me," she said, and I reached over and held both her hands, and she all but walked out of the lake and into the boat.

She said, "Look at you. You're shaking. I've frightened you something terrible." And the next thing I knew we were sitting side by side on the center seat, as if rowing together we could make better time getting back, and maybe build a fire in the fireplace and sip some wine or, even better, some brandy, a blanket draped across my shoulders and back.

And the truth is that I have, in fact, done exactly that, though certainly not in the LaVanns' cabin, but rather in my own, on another lake in another state, and with a woman my age who became my wife for a time. A good twenty years after Mrs. LaVann said, "Shall we stay then for a few more minutes while you calm down?"

I had no idea how late it was, or how long it would be before we'd be packing the car to head home, me and Darwin in the back seat, the two of us silent and staring out at whatever zoomed by on opposite sides of the road, while Mr. LaVann glanced back at me in the rearview.

"Look, Wayne," Mrs. LaVann said. "There's the Goat Fish." And then she pointed above the lake's south end and said, "And there's the Double Ship," as if the sky were a sea, and we were mariners charting a course to who knows where. "There—the Wreath of Flowers," she said. "The Lover's Knot . . . the Dragon's Tail."

Our heads were touching, and her wet hair stuck to my right cheek. The sky was clear. Back then I couldn't differentiate one star from another, though I understood them to be millions and millions of light-years away.

I SAW DARWIN just one time after he and his dad moved downstate. As I did, too. First for college, where I earned a degree in fisheries from the University of Michigan, and then to work for the Michigan Department of Natural Resources, where I am still employed. I'm single again and have two children, a daughter and a son. They're nine and eleven. We—my ex and I—share joint custody, and most weekends during July and late into August they spend time with me at the cottage I bought a few years back. It's a fairly short drive from where they live with their mother, with whom I'm cordial. For a while we even considered getting back together, a second go-around, but the outcome seemed so clearly forgone—and no one, especially the children, needed to go through that again. We care for and trust each other, and that's another kind of love.

If anything, she believes me to be overly protective. Our kids, Delaney and Gregory, are not named after my parents, who against the odds are still together. My mom is still wrestling with her demons, and my dad has finally grown tired of railing against the world's inability to measure up.

AGAIN THIS YEAR, before I drained the pipes and closed up the cottage for winter, the kids and I rowed out, as we always do, to a spot we know, and I slowly let down the anchor. The kids, wearing wet-suit vests and snorkel masks, slid quietly, one after the other, into the lake to float motionless above a massive trunk, its branches alive with snagged plugs and lures, a few of them mine. The tackle tree is what we call it, and the water there is ten or twelve feet deep and clear as a well.

I made a show of drawing into my lungs all the air they can hold. "I'll be right back," I said. "Don't you guys go anywhere." And they both smiled and nodded.

When finally I kicked my fins and dove, baitfish flashed and scattered everywhere around me, as though we were on a reef, the hovering sun weightless on my children's backs. Instead of a knife strapped to my leg, I carried a pair of miniature sewing scissors to snip the tangled leaders at the swivels and collected what I could: a Johnson Silver Minnow, a Rooster Tail, a shiny chartreuse Krocodile. A Berkley Power Worm that twisted and wiggled as if it was alive.

Then came my favorite part of all: looking up and watching the slow-motion rise of my air bubbles toward those two sets of wide-open eyes, magnified behind their masks. They've got their mother's eyes — bright blue — and my dark hair, and the way they breathed so easily through their snorkels made them sound as if they were dreaming, arms outflung in free fall.

AFTER THEY'RE IN BED and asleep I'll sometimes turn off all the lights and stand just outside the front door to stare across to the far end of the lake. Maybe sip a cold beer and be alert for shooting stars, feeding fish, voices that just might trail back on a certain current or breeze. Women and boys and time gone missing, gone elsewhere, gone lost.

And this: I have listened to migrating snow geese fly toward a moon as thin and silver as a hook. I'm forty-two. I band blackbirds whose molten gold irises glow with the fury of fanned embers, and I get paid to stay watchful and record how many return. The miles and the months, and whatever that passage might tell us.

ALL THE
TIME
IN THE
WORLD

MY FATHER'S NAME IS BRADLEY CHICKY. He who fanned fifteen consecutive batters to win the 1989 Division II high school state championship. A spider-arm southpaw submariner whose full-ride scholarships mark this town's first-ever big-league prospect.

Except that it's the new millennium, the year 2004, and so long gone are those glory days that just this morning he gripped the baseball's tight red seams in the double hook of his prosthetic to demonstrate how to throw "No, not a downer, a sinker," as he said. "And here—like this for a heater, like this for a splitter, okay? Got that?" As if right out of left field, the blue mid-November twilight snow falling, I'd decided to try out for some latter-day version of A *League of Their Own.*

No matter the weather he'll sometimes play catch in the backyard with his girlfriend Lyndel, who stops by certain evenings after work. If I decide to hike those couple miles instead of riding the school bus, there they are when I get home, two silhouettes in the semidarkness. She hasn't spent the night at our house, nor he at her place, and I assume it's for my sake that they're taking things slow. We're up to twice each week that the three of us sit down to dinner, the extra leaf just recently reinserted into the dining room table. She might, as he maintains, *be* a dynamite Chef Boyardee, but bite-wise I take maybe one or two and, blank-faced, lower my fork to the plate and excuse myself without a single word. They haven't yet, but if either of them attempts to coerce me back, I swear I'll yank that new linen tablecloth from underneath the serving platters and silverware, the ceramic gravy boat, and those oversize glasses of ice water like some irate and vengeful magician.

He says to give her a chance; she's a good sport, spirited. A real game-changer is how he puts it, a welcome addition. Plus she's plenty smart, he says, reads a ton, and has a two-year degree in health and fitness from the local community college. "In time you'll grow to like her, Sam," he says.

"Right," I say.

But nothing deters his enthusiasm, her painted fingernails flashing signs and my father bent over at the waist and staring in as she squats and rocks back on her heels, her ass mere inches from the half-frozen ground, a Detroit Tigers ball cap worn backward, as if that's cool. Sometimes she takes off the catcher's mitt and warms both hands in her armpits. She shrugs and shivers and yet acts as if this is the most fun she's had in decades. Home plate is maybe fifteen yards from where, in full windup, he releases the ball, every pitch a slow, looping changeup though he claims that some scout's speed gun once clocked him at 101 mph. Other times he'll practice his pick-off move, his sneaky slide step. All of it, under our current circumstances, about a bazillion light years removed from the majors.

Anyway, Lyndel teaches Pilates and yoga at Go Figure, so *hers* is pretty much perfect in that camo sports bra and short-shorts getup she occasionally wears, a shiny silver bracelet on either wrist like handcuffs. Standing straight-legged she can touch both elbows to the floor, fingers folded like she's praying, and then hold that pose before tucking under herself as if she might push all the way up past her own backside, like something out of a Chinese circus. She's twenty-six, seven years younger than my father and a full eight years older than my mom was when she had me—Samantha Ann. Or, as that sheriff's department deputy I hand my urine sample to every other Saturday afternoon always singsongs, "Sam Chicky, Sam Chicky," like he's propositioning some teenage junkie slut, which so isn't me.

I mean, against the odds I'm holding it together, doing my best, resisting every temptation, and avoiding lockup by side-sailing as fast and far away from the local pot and meth heads as possible. Staying clean. And stripped naked not a single body piercing or the fancy needlework of some butt-crack tattoo. No hickeys, either, ditto the eyeliner, and the sad fact is that foreplay thus far pretty much constitutes locking fingers with a guy.

But just one time, when Deputy Dildo orders me to empty my pockets and sweatshirt pouch, I imagine, among my personal and lawful contents, having enough nerve to plant a couple of Trojan Ultra Thins. Packets I could flip right onto the counter. Free samples from the Journey Church for safe, underage sex is what I'd offer up, an inside joke between me and my best friend Allison. Maybe bat my eyes and nod toward the empty holding cell, the stripped down cot, but like my father reminds me, "Zip it. Keep your motor mouth shut and your thoughts to yourself." To ensure that I arrive there on time, he's the one who chaperones me in his pickup. He rolls down the window, leans his head against the seat rest, his hook visoring above his already closed eyes, and says, as I exit, "Remember, no attitude, right? Do you hear me? No bullshit this time."

My official guilty-as-charged? Random theft and alcohol. As in every morning before school, my father in the shower, I'd refill the same juice box with straight Bombay Sapphire from the secret survival stash in my closet. Then during third-hour phys ed, I'd sip between sets of stomach crunches and jumping jacks, and the one time I puked the gym teacher thought it was food poisoning or the flu and called my father at work to come pick me up.

I haven't lapsed in almost three months and counting, and the NO ENTRY sign on my bedroom door I removed voluntarily. Not that he'd walk in unannounced one way or the other. It's the tone, as my father says, the negative message it sends. Sort of like how I used to gnaw on ballpoint after ballpoint until the spring broke and the ink erupted inside my mouth. Now I take notes instead, and my grades, as of just last week, they're back up again above average. Nothing *Quiz Bowl* or *Odyssey of the Mind*. Nothing, as my teachers make clear, that even approximates my full potential, though so far no backslide, either, and so no more hassles and scare tactics from the school principal and guidance counselor about having to repeat the year.

But three sheets flapping I'll shoplift almost anything spur of the moment: a silk blouse, more booze, Elmer's and Magic Markers to uncap and sniff all day. Rubber cement. Model airplane glue. Bottles of syrupy Robitussin as chasers. Once, a chew toy and a couple packs of liver chips, plus a Basenji pup to feed them to. Scooped up in broad daylight from Spoiled Brats, our Front Street pet shop that's likely, like so many of the town's landmark mom-and-pops, to turn belly-up, the census here being in perpetual long-term free fall.

I named the pooch Ty Cobb, for my father's all-time favorite ballplayer. An innocent, warm-blooded addition to the household that we could love and care for together and spoil rotten in my mom's absence. We'd never had a pet. Not so much as a goldfish or gerbil, and when my father, bleary-eyed, home finally at the tail-end of another fifty-hour workweek at the foundry, offered his dead hand to be licked and sniffed, the puppy peed right there on the living room carpet. "I'll clean it up," I said, and the first words out his mouth: "Why didn't you just leave our names and phone number and address? And hand over a note saying, *BEWARE: KLEPTOMANIAC ON THE PREMISES?*"

"Maybe I bought him," I said. "Did you ever consider that?" And he said back, "Tell it to the judge," and then he threatened to press charges himself and wave bye-bye as the juvenile-delinquent facility van pulled away. He'd had it, he said. "Enough is enough, Sam. The dog's got papers, a high-dollar price tag, and there's no buying you out of this. Not after the fact, and I don't even want to. Listen:

this isn't kid's stuff anymore, a pound or rescue mutt; we're talking a felony offense. Do you understand what that means, the possible consequences? Trust me, you've just taken on way more than you ever bargained for. And God forbid that I lose you, too."

He sat me down at the kitchen table and coached me, sentence by sentence, as I composed what sounded to my ears like a heart-felt letter of apology and remorse. Still woozy and half hungover, I took a while to get the words "appealing for clemency" unslurred, but the cops, they'd already been summoned anyway, a good hour in advance of that written admission of guilt. The final period, the "Sincerely yours," the scribbled, almost illegible, back-slanting left-handed signature I'd sometimes practice in the back row of every class to annihilate another wasted few seconds of mandatory school time—all of it made little difference.

"SHE DOES IT FOR ATTENTION." That's what the first Family Services social worker—young and nervous and strictly by the numbers—con-cluded. A rookie, as my father insists. Limited. Right or wrong, she attributed such aberrant behavior to my mom's midnight departure eight months earlier, and to my on-the-rebound father still somewhat tilty in *his* thinking. Like I told her, he and I, we do our best to tune each other out and, whenever possible, communicate telepathically or in single-word sentences. "*Sorry*" is not among them, except, I guess, whenever I attempt to decipher the Morse code of his hook tap-tapping on the Naugahyde couch cushion as he watches the His-tory Channel or *60 Minutes* with the sound turned off.

Around Lyndel I'm occasionally more forthcoming and way less inclined to play the victim, the angry, uppity, unstable, at-risk, inso-lent, wayward, and all-mixed-up crazy child—"the offending minor," as the juvenile court judge referred to me. I'm also less inclined to lay the blame so directly on my parents, or on anyone else for that matter. And for sure I *don't blame* Lyndel, who I first off figured for a ditz I could easily despise, my every silent glare announcing, "I can wait you out. This is not your house. There is no later on, no better tomorrows here. This is who we are. Leave now."

Truth be told she's okay, with no grubbing up or big-sister stupid stuff. No offers of a free radical Jazzercise class or any personal trainer tips to improve my bust line or ease the pain of those killer premenstrual cramps and spasms. And her laugh . . . it's eerie-weird in the extreme, like a fun gene long dormant in this dysfunctional family. Zero rug rats and never married. When I finally asked her what's the deal here anyway—my father chasing after the young stuff—she said, her jeans low-slung, her hair blue-black and shiny, "Lyndel, not Lolita." Which I didn't get, but I winced when she added, "Your dad is a good man at a bad time and half out of his mind with worry over you."

I'm fifteen and by far the tallest girl in the entire school. At twelve I stood an even six feet in my mom's high heels and magenta lipstick and had a premonition of myself as Miss Michigan-turned-runway-supermodel and swinging five-hundred-dollar handbags. Leggy and gray-eyed like my father and, reformed or not, I don't for one second assume that I'm the only guilty party here whenever he asks, all pissed off and judgmental, "How brainless can you be?" I, too, lose all composure and fire right back, exactly like my mom used to do, the same zinger about how he'd forfeited a life of fame and fortune and, as she said, for what, one goddamn dark night of the soul's idea of a joke?

"Beyond belief" is how she'd phrase it, and my standing comeback to my dad was, "Yeah, remember that?"

"Every day," he says. "Every last painful detail." He means the homemade guillotine and that forged steel doorframe he hauled out of the county dump. Pulleys and half a dozen oblong window weights, and the side-by-side outhouse shitter holes sawed crosswise and hinged like a double yoke to fit those frail, pale, aristocratic necks of Louis XVI and Marie Antoinette. A last-ditch, hands-on world history show-and-tell he brainstormed to salvage a final passing grade so he could graduate and they could flee to Florida or Arizona or Texas: no-hitters, perfect games, a College World Series MVP ring, and trophies enough to fill a hallway of polished glass cases. Jerseys and scoreboards and pennant flags to autograph. My mom, already pregnant with me, could follow the team bus in that white Mustang convertible she imagined was already theirs and think about the sprawling brick ranch or split-level they'd buy, the backyard in-ground swimming pool with its rainbow of underwater lights, and a trampoline. And eggs any style.

All of which sure beat, she said, slow-dying here in this squatty, spawned-out, northern Michigan shithole of a town where they married anyhow, for better or for worse, and honeymooned in a cheap rustic cabin just a few miles south. And where some twisted turn of fate determined that I, too, would be born and raised.

"Let it rest," my father would say, his name stitched in red cursive above his work-shirt pocket. "Good God Almighty, do we always have to end up at the same damn crash site?" My mom, each and every time she'd wig out or fly into overwind—didn't really matter anymore what for—insisted that the moment was forever fixed in her memory. The bedroom walls, they're so tin-can thin that I've awakened nights to screams unlike anything you've ever heard unless, as she'd say, you've witnessed close up a human arm lopped clean off below the elbow in a public school classroom.

"You couldn't make it up"—that's what the local newscasts reported as far across the Big Lake as La Crosse and Fargo. Freak of freaks. Grimmer than grim. Referring to him, all six-foot-six, as the next Big Unit but with his career closed out just like that. "You don't want to hear this," they said, as if it might incite or traumatize young athletes everywhere, and then they provided a graphic play-by-play anyway. The teacher present—"My God, the magnitude," the news anchors intoned in hushed voices—his teammates and his teenage fiancée all gathered for the execution, laughing and hooting and slapping him on the back, and then, as if in stop-time, looking on in horror.

They mentioned how he'd done his homework. His stand-up easel and flip chart and a gabble of gruesome facts about the French Revolution: how king and queen were beheaded separately in 1793, His Majesty in January and she in October, a child bride, barely fourteen when they tied the royal knot.

"Jailbait," my mom—her baby bump already showing—interrupted from the front of the classroom. "Cradle robber." My father then explained, to her and to everyone, that if he could have he'd have spared the queen's life and maybe changed the violent course of history. But this was now or never, and all that mattered was to pass the class, a measly C-minus their gateway to the future, and what was theirs right there for the taking.

"And Jesus Christ Almighty," my mom said, wherever he'd found the mannequins, the padded church kneeler, was beyond hers or anyone's comprehension. Not to mention those flowing indigo robes. Coconuts for heads, faces sandpapered smooth and spray-painted white and pasty like geishas', that on this day two centuries later would tumble and roll together—their carved pink lips barely parted, blindfolds refused and their doomed eyes neither closed nor staring downward in disgrace but rather looking straight ahead.

By all accounts they were still crazy about each other, my father ad-libbed, as if the case for true love at any age might invalidate all those trumped-up and treasonous charges. They admitted to nothing, he said, and right to the bitter end remained poised and silent, resilient and unafraid.

Then came a drum roll, and my father prepared the honed and weighted industrial paper-cutter blade, way too heavy for a single release lever and a makeshift shear pin. But even still, as my mom calculates, what were the odds, the prospects of such an ungodly, unforgiving physics, that it would snap full force exactly as my father reached in to straighten those two wavy white wigs borrowed from the drama club?

FAMILY SERVICES SOCIAL WORKER NUMBER TWO—older, seasoned, the pack's dominant jackal with the focused determination of breaking through to me alive in her eyes. A veteran, according to my father, a prime-time, no-nonsense professional. They've talked, and a few times all three of us together have sat down. He says for me to pay attention, that this one knows her stuff, a warning that she's seen it all—every defiant, cocky, headstrong young screw-up like yours truly. Her square Army-green coffee mug says, SPEAK YOUR MIND, but whenever I offer an opinion she wide-eyes me with the emptiest, most remote, and most dismissive stare in creation. Glowers like she can see right through me from the onset to the absolute end of my socially impaired and substandard existence. Nods. Clenches up. Says stuff like, "So." Says, "Uh-huh. Fair enough, though the victims of much greater calamities cope and move on, don't they?" Always slams on the brakes with some loaded, instant-override question like that. Then says, "Go on, please." As in, "Sing it again, Sam, and let's see where *this* next burnout version of reality leads us, shall we?"

We somehow forge our slow way hourward. It's all part of the guilty plea, and of me being perceived not as some dangerous criminal but rather as not really giving a shit. So mostly I just tuck in, nod and grimace and gut-roll through every session. I close my eyes. With my finest fakery I stammer and bite my lip and sometimes cry because it's a thin ledge I'm walking—that's the message loud and clear—and the falloff rate for girls my age is nothing to frigging underestimate. I'm good at this: hand tremors and hyperventilating on demand. Within seconds I can double my pulse rate and begin to run a fever. Wicked sweats and hiccups, and the whole act so convincing that I once said Hollywood when she asked about potential career tracks, and she didn't for one dense second even catch the irony. Talk about a movie set on Venus or Mars.

Her name's Ms. Foisie. Early forty-something, springy strawberry-blond locks drawn back into a ponytail. Perfume so thick that you enter the room and boom, a giant blast of Chocolate Daisy or Autumn Snakeroot explodes straight up through your nostrils. And those eyes, I swear, wide-spaced and lobelia blue, and the pupils black as dahlias. Feather earrings to top it off. I've never admitted as much, but it's enough to get a person high. For that initial full hour of "getting to know you," I kept scanning the room for bumblebees and humming-birds, a praying mantis maybe. The featured talk that day was all about my parents and the recklessness of teenage sex and marriage. "You do," she said, "understand what I'm telling you, correct?"

I nodded. "The basic thrust," I said, and she said, "Which is?" and I said, "Things happen. Things buzz"—but hey, not to worry, no lick and stick from where I rest my weary bones and noggin. And look, no engagement rock. I was *still* patiently waiting to go all wild and wet in my dreams, I told her. It's why my father reams me out about the wisecracking. "A curse or spell," he says, but pure reflex is what it actually is, totally spontaneous and, come on, only meant as a joke. All in good fun, woman to woman to possibly lighten the psychic load just a little, and her husband and two sons smiling sideways at me from out of that fancy, gold-leafed photo on her desk.

ALLISON SAYS, "No sweat." Says, "Remember, we're good." Says, "Hey, guess what?" and we simultaneously flip each other off. This goes back to the carnival fortune-teller two summers ago, who held my hand and explained that the length of a woman's middle finger predicts her future. I'd be some modern-day Egyptian queen, all satin clad, dripping rubies and sapphires, ruddering down the Nile at twilight while dining with sheiks or whatever, instead of serving breakfast for minimum wage at our local Denny's.

I whirled around in a full circle on my tiptoes right outside the gypsy tent with its heavy canvas flaps and burning candles and Mason jars of giant scorpions and smiling horseshoe bats in formaldehyde. I said, "Holy rip-shit," confirming that wherever in the hemispheres the spirit took us was where *we* were headed, nonstop into the slipstream of epic romance and greatness and maybe even a blockbuster feature-length film or two, with Oscars and Golden Globes. And so we made that pact to go and go as we sashayed arm in arm in our skintight miniskirts and flip-flops through the slowly rising mist of the midway—what my mom called the land of stuffed lions and lambs, and that prized oversize panda she insisted nobody ever won: "Nobody, Sam. Remember that. Above all else, remember that when the fairyland dream smoke clears, women like us, like you and me, we always, every single solitary time, wake up elsewhere. And that other life we wanted so badly? The one back *there*? It's nothing more than a mirage, the simple-sad story of our botched and misguided lives."

What I now believe is that my father trying and trying to prove my mother wrong about him actually made her love him less. The ring toss, that pyramid of milk bottles that never wobbled or fell and in her eyes rendered him a mere figment of his former self.

THE POSTMARK on her last few letters is from Kenosha. They're addressed to me and me alone, and to my knowledge she's made no other human contact hereabouts. I could lie, tell my father, "Mom asked about you. How you were doing." But what she's conveyed thus far is this: in her new job she individually hand-wraps brandy-soaked chocolates in a warehouse where they pipe in *Peter and the Wolf*, and musicals like *The Sound of Music*, and Judy Garland's "Over the Rainbow."

I've thought for the millionth time, *Just hop a Trailways, Sam.* It would have been a done deal long ago had she ever once offered to take me with her. Or had she, after the fact, dropped the slightest hint that the choice was mine, legal or otherwise. Or had she said of course she wants me to move out there or, bare minimum, to come visit for an extended stay—though yes, it's too late for this Thanksgiving, but consider Christmas as a possibility, okay?

She says the Salvation Army ringers are already at it with their handbells and hanging red coin kettles. And the tree on top of the water tower is decorated with ten thousand translucent stars, a galaxy of tiny blue spires aglow in the night sky. If only she had a balcony or fire escape, she thinks, she could see the display from her single-occupancy efficiency apartment. It's small, of course, but has a TV and a microwave and a minifridge.

She says, "Can you imagine it, a town with prehistoric sturgeon in the rivers? Caviar!" she says. And a brand-new Grand Union that hires the blind as greeters, as well as to stand at the head of every other aisle to offer toothpicks and so much free sample food that it's impossible for anyone to go hungry. So far not word one about another man in her life, though that's how she's ended up where she has, morose and alone, lost to us. That's the part I hate her for and refuse to forgive. Except that I haven't, against my father's will and certainty, ruled out entirely that she still might rally like someone suddenly waking from a decade-long coma and remembering her husband's name, the address and phone number where she used to live. Or like the mute who picks up a smoky cat's-eye marble or piece of mica, holds it to the sun, and begins to lip-sync some long-forgotten serenade about leaving and love—and then just dodges the holy, haphazard hell right out of there and straight for home.

Instead, she claims that the haloed prison lights she drives by some nights remind her how lucky she is to be so free and alive. Though possibly it's a lunatic asylum, she can't be positive—the grilled windows and the like—but either way it's just another case in point, as my father would argue, to fortify his position against her ever returning.

That's true. It's like she's writing from a land so foreign and far-flung I had to locate it on our Rand McNally atlas just to remind myself she's only in Wisconsin: a straight shot north through the UP and then, at any given junction or crossroads, just hang a louie and hold that sightline all the way to the horizon.

What's clear to everyone is that if she hadn't in fits and flashes beat it out of here so often, we'd *already* be on our way to rescue her, whispering, "Where are you, where are you?" and then begging her back.

First time she fled was on foot, and my father found her shivering in the predawn just blocks away, silent and shamefaced, her eyes closed like she'd been slapped. And then him leading her by the hand slowly past the neighbors' houses, up our porch stairs with the dying potted spider plants, and back inside. Once a regular homebody, she began disappearing, no telling when or where to, a half mile or so beyond the town's outskirts to begin with, and later she got stranded out by the I-75 motor lodge where that grid of high-tension wires crackles and hums. And that was followed not long after by collect calls from Menominee and Battle Creek, though never before had she crossed state lines or stayed gone for more than a day or two, a week at most. But this time, come spring, it'll mark a calendar year—and by then, according to my father, she'll have forfeited all rights, including visitation privileges.

He says about having filed for divorce, "How wrong you are. We've done everything we can. Everything humanly possible, Sam. There's no turning back, not anymore, and your mother and me, we've *already* gone our separate ways. No other alternative exists, and for sure no coping or compromising away what she *imagined* and believed back then should've been our lives going forward."

What *I* imagine is her vanishing, not for months or even years, but forever. And the only photograph in my possession is a grainy, 8x10 black and white my father secretly snapped of her like some private eye, while she stood staring skyward into the storm light as it massed and rumbled tidal-like directly toward her. The air seems electrified and a giant monochrome shadow eclipses those endless windswept alfalfa fields—the entire silvery span of them. Her head is flung back and her arms are outstretched as if, as he reported it back then, she was waiting to be abducted by aliens.

"It's who she is," he said. "A human lost and found and lost, and, for good measure, gone, and gone lost yet again. Elsewhere—that's the direction she's always been headed in. The sequel to the sequel to the sequel, Sam. Look," he said, as he handed me the photo. "Look at this. Look closely and tell me honestly that you or anyone can conceive for her a happier outcome."

Ms. Foisie agrees. As she's said repeatedly, "Let's let the credits roll, shall we?" Her take is that my mom suffers from a chronic case of arrested development, the defections so numerous that even I had to admit that I'd lost count. But hope, nonetheless, springs eternal, right? "And she is, after all," I've continued to argue, "still my mom. Is she not?" And Ms. Foisie's standard comeback is, "Yes, she who has self-destructively turned your lives into a charade," implying furthermore that she'd turned me into my own worst enemy.

I suppose I could have revealed, but wouldn't ever to the likes of her, how some nights my mom would sit on the end of my bed and patiently cast whichever hand shadows I requested, animal or reptile or insect. Rabbits, dragonflies, camels and storks and pelicans. Sometimes that scary profile of a crocodile, her index and middle fingers slowly scissoring up and down, while that raised knuckle of an eye socket floated across the calm, imaginary white water of my bedroom wall. How it was me who held the flashlight, who aimed the beam as if it were a magic lantern. How it took two hands and all *ten* fluttery fingers for her to simulate the erratic nose-diving flights of those swallows that nested in the rafters of our unused woodshed. And how one time my mom said, right out of the blue, "No, your father *can't* do this," which was exactly what I'd been wondering. And then, turning to look at me, she speculated that if his double hook was diamond-tipped he'd score each windowpane and tap out a thousand perfect pinpoints to let in the moon and the starlight.

MY FATHER CALLS it the best Christmas present ever, that I've been taken off probation for good behavior. Or possibly, as Allison speculates, the judge was doubling down on my redemption in this, the season of miracles. Either way, as of this weekend, this very Friday night, I've been rewarded with an eleven o'clock curfew. "On the dot and not a second later," my father said, and if the roads start to get bad I'm to head home immediately. They already almost are, though suddenly it seems like we've got all the time in the world.

Because Allison has graduated from learner's permit to driver's license, we're sitting on the front bumper of her parents' second car, a dented, high-mileage Oldsmobile Custom Cruiser, recently tuned-up and with four new snow tires. Plus a first-aid kit and emergency roadside flares—all fizz without the firecracker—stashed in the trunk.

The early pardon calls for a celebration. As Allison says, "Out the door and on the loose like old times. Only better." I agree wholeheartedly now that we're much older, wiser, and wilier, and have wrangled a set of wheels and a full tank of gas, notwithstanding that there's absolutely nowhere to go in weather like this. It's why we're bundled up against the freezing cold, scarves and hats and a Hudson Bay blanket around our skinny shoulders like a double cape. The snow is slow but steady-falling in giant feathery flakes—a scrim half-obscuring the lights of the town below us, the abandoned gravel pits with the rusted-out derricks and the limestone quarry beyond. The only color is the blurry, rectangular, neon-red Dairy Queen sign. Otherwise, everything's white, the pines and Doug firs on the steep downward slant ghosting over, and the foundry smokestack—though we can't see it—like a vertical ice tunnel into the sky.

Months. That's how much winter's ahead. And yet there's not a single county plow taking notice. And no wind at all, and even when we strain to hear that unmistakable shrill whine of transport trailers out on the interstate, we can't. Everything's quiet, the loudest sound anywhere the tips of our two cigarettes burning back with every inhale.

We've been parked for maybe half an hour at this scenic, no-name lovers' lane overlook, but of course no one besides us is around. No jocks on the prowl, but girls like us, we take it on faith that some night hence we will draw them out of their small-town, shit-box lives in droves and teach them how to love us. How to kiss and kiss us all over until their lips and tongues go numb. How to follow the sway of our hips gliding us like phantoms across dream fields so vast that even a search party of thousands couldn't detect a single trace.

Instead, here we are, waylaid in the panorama of so much emptiness that Allison tilts her head heavenward. She says, "Hey, Sam, we gotta go," but even so she leans back against the hood and closes her eyes and remains silent. The snow sticks to her long lashes like tiny white wings; her face is almost luminous. We are beautiful, is what I think, travelers momentarily stranded inside the closed-off borderlands beyond which lie our future lives. I imagine my father standing and staring out the living room window, conjuring a blizzard, thinking about how the winter roads will begin to narrow and the Black Creek Bridge we have to cross to get back, always the first to ice over. He'll switch on the porch light and the TV weather station. He'll call Allison's house to see if we're there, the car's colossal ass end fishtailed safely up the gradual incline of their driveway.

And I imagine my mom, listening to that din of voices inside her head, the fade-ins and fade-outs, the New Year almost upon us, and my overdue trip to visit her never taken, the time we've spent apart growing longer and longer by the day.

"Look," I say. The moon is almost full, and for those delayed few seconds before the snow falls harder into the dark, the disappearing landscape turns purplish blue. "Like a dying spotlight," I say, and this is a pageant, a dance we do while opening the car doors and sliding in. The engine catches on the very first try, the wipers clearing the windshield with one wide swoop. We're ready to launch, and the Olds is no longer a car, as Allison says. It's a catamaran, and the roads are rivers. You can see in the low beams how slowly we're drifting over the snow, leaving no wake. No stars to follow home, though for now, for this night, it is where we're headed.

CALCHECK
AND
PRIEST

CALCHECK WAS ON THE SAW but the chain needed sharpening, the bar already scorched and beginning to smoke. No earplugs or safety goggles, and the laces of his steel-toed boots dragging underfoot. Not to mention that he'd been drinking, possibly for much of the night, and so talk about frigging deranged enough to walk up on the likes of us the way they did just after first light? Two of them, deer hunters in blaze orange, rifles cradled in their arms.

That they were none too happy was difficult to miss, but better them, I thought, than some eager-beaver C.O., given that we'd been cutting all fall on state land without a permit, determined to put up a few more cords for the vast and not so magical season ahead. We'd both harvested a decent buck during the bow season—a six- and an eight-point, and our freezers looked pretty respectable: vacuum-sealed venison roasts and chops and steaks and burger, ribs for the smoker—and so we hadn't paid all that much attention to the firearms opener.

Nor to a lot of stuff lately, preoccupied as we'd been with other more serious matters. Like plotting to rescue Calcheck's former girl-friend's eight-year-old son, once we located their whereabouts. All that we'd so far pieced together was that the kid's mother had likely hooked up with her loser ex-husband at the Tangled Antler, where she'd been waitressing nights. If not the ex, then someone she'd known in another lifetime foreign to us.

"Maybe Canada?" the bartender said, like he'd spun a globe and his index fingertip had stopped on Saskatoon or Winnipeg. He said, "Real strange looking. Fake smile, shitty teeth. Weird. Fucked-up skinny and hyper and asked right off for her section, and next thing her drink order's up and I'm calling her name but nothing. Doglegged it out the side door's all I could figure. Him, too. There one minute, gone the next. But no question—for sure she knew he'd be there. No way was it some spur-of-the-moment thing."

After that the trail went dead in a hurry. That, although I didn't say so at the time, was probably just as well, given that Calcheck was not the kid's father. Bore no physical resemblance whatsoever, and legal guardianship did not seem to me like the logical end result of abduction. Given that the courts were the courts, and the very last place either one of us needed to revisit.

I'd come close on occasion but hadn't thus far served any jail time. Rinky-dink plea deals and community service and a noncombative, low-key demeanor that I'd inherited from my old man. Meaning that *I* was the one you wanted troubleshooting a potentially explosive situation, such as being blindsided at close range by two total strangers standing shoulder to shoulder and glaring wild-eyed at us with undisguised outrage and contempt.

Calcheck's finger was on the trigger, and I flashed on him lifting the chainsaw above his head with one hand, like some crazed Rambo rage-firing an M60 into the great gray heart of the northern Michigan sky. It was exactly the kind of thing he'd do if he felt put upon, the kind of thing he had done, without much consideration or concession as to whether the response had, before or after the fact, been justified one way or another.

"Morning," I said, but not so much as a nod in return. Instead, they just stood there, squinting and sizing us up. Jaw muscles clenched and their mouths open just enough for each next breath to plume and eddy sideways in the almost imperceptible breeze. There were maybe two inches of snow on the ground, and so we could see from what direction they'd stalked up on us.

"That's correct. We're set up right over there on the backside of that first rise. And what we'd like to know—what we're trying real hard to wrap our heads around—is how, exactly, does it happen with a forest this size that you boys decide to fire up not fifty yards from our blinds?" He looked off, as if to allow his eyes to recalibrate and, on the reverse swing back to us, find only woods and trees. "For fucksake," he said. "It's the opening goddamn day of the season."

"That true?" I said, and glanced at Calcheck, who winced, like, "Hoo, boy, how the hell did we blank on that?" I guess we hadn't—not really. I mean even the mill had shut down, as if November fifteenth were a national holiday, and WELCOME HUNTERS signs hung in every restaurant and party store window in the county, bullet holes through the heart of every speed limit sign on the town's outskirts. And talk about landing a vacant motel room; you'd score better odds for Key West in late February, where the women—or so I'd heard—walked the streets in bikinis and flip-flops. But the truth was—and for all the deer sign back in where we were—we'd never before encountered a human.

Late-forties, max, and downstate or out of state seemed a safe and reasonable assumption. And plenty pissed and in possession of serious weaponry. So I underhanded the splitting maul in a couple of slow-looping, top-heavy rotations toward the ass end of the pickup, its tailgate down, and said, "Hey, our oversight. We'll pack right up and be out of your way. No problem."

It was Friday, the weekend looming, and to try and lighten the mood I quoted my old man who, no matter how discouraging the outcome of whatever we'd pursued—be it shooting ducks or geese or spearing suckers or pike—would say, "The good news, Oden?" And I'd say back, "Yup, to live is to fight another day."

"Four," the mouthy one amended, fuming now. "That's how long we're up for. *Four* days, though we can shit kiss this first one good-bye, wouldn't you agree?" He shook his head, extra slow motion, and said, "Listen. Do yourselves a favor and don't show up here again. Don't go doing that dumb thing, you hear?" He said, "Beyond dumb, that's what this is," and I hoped he wouldn't push the cheap talk past that.

Like we'd trespassed their private hunting preserve. Or had any inkling that they existed anywhere in the world. Much less off an abandoned bunkered-out two-track, where even the undercarriage of Calcheck's beat-to-hell, jacked-up, four-wheel-drive Toyota slammed down full-force, no matter how slowly you drove in or out, tree branches snapping and bullwhipping the windshield. We'd even had to use the winch a time or two to get unstuck.

We were into the eleventh straight day since Sherri-Lynn had up and vanished without a word or a note, leaving most of her belongings behind. But not the emergency cash fund set aside for the guaranteed calamities that winter in a small border town never failed to provide. Savings she'd most likely snort away in a string of fleabags somewhere. Traveling light and fast was my take, though Calcheck wanted to believe, or at least half-believe, that she'd be back, but of course that hadn't transpired, and the damage seemed to me a project beyond repair. And which, bare-knuckled, he'd taken out on the gatepost out front of his trailer house. What Sherri-Lynn referred to as the blue tunnel, or sometimes the shoebox or the torpedo, ever since he'd weather-stripped and covered the north-facing windows with plastic sheeting.

The kind of place with two heavy-duty slide bolts on the inside of the windowless metal door, just in case the wrong people came knocking. A place it was easy to imagine standing empty, and it had been briefly before he bartered his carpentry and plumbing and electrical skills for a year's free rent. When that expired, he exercised his option to purchase; it was a fixer-upper and moneywise not a terrible investment to get tied down by, especially if you intended to stay around for a while, there being nothing in the immediate or even foreseeable future to drive up the real estate prices.

Still, the property included a sizeable outbuilding, a Quonset that he'd shored up and converted into a wood shop with a gas generator in case of a power outage. Six acres that backed up to state land, a double row of mature windbreak red pines and a decent-sized cold-water creek running through. Plus a fire ring out back, with a grill on top and four stump seats, and a cooler of frosties that we kept well stocked during the summer months. Like I told Calcheck, anyone covets a private and quiet and trimmed-down lifestyle off the beaten path, they've probably set their sights correctly.

And I meant it, though what registered first thing when Sherri-Lynn moved in was trouble, the latest round of bad news to fall our way. To be fair, I'd recently bungled a romance with a woman, and a homely kind of hard-luck beauty seemed like just another phase or direction into that same messy dead end. That same doomed-from-the-start fucked-up story—a chronic affliction that plagued men like us, who were inward and weak-willed when it involved the extended absence of female company, a warm and willing body to tuck up next to during the wee hours.

If asked to state my name for the record and swear on the Good Book to tell the whole truth and nothing but, I'd admit that I did indeed some evenings sit up and take notice of Sherri-Lynn's skin-tight, off-the-shoulder tanks in every color of the rainbow, one for every next lonely night of the week. Not that I wouldn't have sat around batching it like old times, drinking and shooting the shit, just me and Calcheck, though for sure she didn't curtail my interest and participation any. We'd hit it off right from the start, and she seemed to enjoy my company, and I never one time had to hunt up subjects to fill even those longer silences when she drifted deeper and deeper into lost-look mode.

Calcheck was one year younger than me. But whereas I'd landed a job at the pulp mill straight out of high school, the day *he* graduated he hitchhiked almost two hundred miles round trip to enlist in the army as an infantry grunt; he also took up boxing. Undersize for a middleweight, he could nonetheless take anyone's best shot, and, standing toe to toe, his eyes bruised purple and swollen shut, he refused to clench or cover up or be KO'd. All balls and tough as nails but also, to my way of thinking, borderline crazy.

I'd seen him fight on half a dozen undercards after he came home. Always at the casinos, what Calcheck called "beyond the white man's law," and where he got paid in greenbacks. We'd drink pretty hard after each bout, win or lose. And then double down at the poker or blackjack table, people moving away when they saw his face, and leaving just the two of us against the house.

One night on quick notice he designated *me* as his cornerman. Like I knew the first damn thing about that. But like Calcheck said, other than from head butts he really wasn't much of a bleeder, and so when the bell rang I said, "Okay, go get 'em, Champ. No mercy. Close the show and let's get out of here." But the guy was a monster, a light heavy, muscled and hulking side to side like a skinned Kodiak, nostrils flared. After a brutal, opening-round pounding, I said, "Stay the fuck on the stool. This is suicide."

"Unless you like to bang and brawl," he said, and smiled, and I slid his mouthpiece back in and ducked under the ropes and over the ring apron, the crowd already on its feet and chanting Calcheck's name as I looked away.

At thirty-five, and in spite of the cigarettes and the booze, he was still in halfway decent shape, unlike the great white hunters before us who'd be on their knees dry-heaving if they teamed up to drag even an average-size doe fifty frigging feet. And I did not, if at all possible, wish them to be the recipients of his fearlessness and his wrath. Not with guns involved, and for sure not with the weight of recent events still foremost on his mind.

I thought, *Okay, just bail out of here. Just play along and walk it back, easy like. Just follow my lead, more or less. For now anyhow.* As if I'd transmitted a silent code Calcheck hit the kill switch, and with his other hand he fished the keys from his pocket and tossed them to me. He held his free palm up and fired off not a single word, as if there really was a first time for everything, and if so, this was the proof of that exact moment.

He'd picked me up early that morning right on time, heater off and the window cracked for a little cold air to help clear his head. He still looked pretty rough and so I left it down, started the engine, and shifted into gear. Even with the saw and splitting maul and gas can bouncing around in the truck bed I could hear a volley of shots in the distance. Calcheck opened the glove box and took out a pint of Old Museum, which he uncapped but didn't right off take a hit. "Yahoos," he said, and put the hood up on his sweatshirt and closed his eyes.

"Flat-out," I said. "With a capital Y," and a capital "Hoo." And although I couldn't, after a few seconds, see them anymore in the rearview, I slid lower in the seat. Calcheck had survived two tours in Iraq, a subject he did not care to talk about, and so I left unmentioned this weird, jittery sensation that the crosshairs of some snipers' rifles were fixed on the backs of our heads.

HE'D HELPED RAISE THE KID for just short of a year and a half, which resulted in Child Protective Services having backed off Sherri-Lynn's ass. Bills were getting paid. She'd cleaned up her act pretty good, meaning the drugs, and there were nights when, playing cards or Monopoly, she seemed happy enough, the lady of the house.

And Priest, her son, had his own room, a TV, and some VHS tapes—*Beetlejuice*, *Edward Scissorhands*, flicks like that. In the backyard—don't ask me how or where from—they had one of those enormous satellite dishes, as if Calcheck were attempting to channel back broadcasts from Pluto or Mars. No kidding, he could mastermind and build just about anything, and when he asked Priest what he wanted for his birthday, he said, "A tree house?" which materialized in under two weeks, an octagon complete with a rope ladder and a trap door and a shiny chrome fireman's pole to slide down.

It used to be, after they first arrived, that the kid would avert his eyes and communicate in sentences that either tapered off into silence or simply quit midway. Not like he was shy or slow-witted or at a loss, but more like he was unaccustomed to adults paying attention to anything he had to say. Couldn't sit still for five seconds, and instead he'd tiptoe from window to window to make sure the coast was clear before he'd go outside alone. But not anymore. He'd stopped wetting his bed, and against Sherri-Lynn's objections Calcheck would crouch and demonstrate for Priest how to set his feet and jab and hook. How to knot his fists, hands held high, and, should the need arise, how to counterpunch with a solid uppercut to the kahunas. What Calcheck called a haymaker from hell.

"And don't ever forget," he said, "the bigger they are," by which he meant, screw a fair fight if need be, because that's where it always started. Always. On the playground during recess, pound for pound, just unload with a fury and watch how fast that Goliath pussy towers down. "One time's all it'll take," Calcheck promised, "and he'll be sleeping with his tail tucked and a pillow between his knees, the fight in him pissed away forever."

I'd once cut the laces on Calcheck's boxing gloves and pulled them off in the dressing room, and when he opened his fists I could see that his fingertips had split open, the bones sticking through like the nubs of bloody talons. "Jesus," I said, his hand wraps like a tangle of stained bandages and gauze. Even then he got up on his toes, did an Ali shuffle, and started shadowboxing in the full-length mirror, as if that phantom opponent staring him down was none other than himself, a busted-up pugilist, all heart, but without sense enough to retire.

His record when he finally *did* throw in the towel? Who cared? A fan favorite, he'd collect his purse, which after licensing and fees was low stakes, though in the local bars more often than not guys would spring for his drinks. Pat him on the back, a journeyman, past-his-prime club fighter who put on a good show, on the back, but I wondered, at what cost? Brain cells scrambled, a nose that jackknifed in two directions and made him look angry and old and deformed. Scar tissue where an eyebrow used to be.

During his career he'd busted all twenty-eight bones if you counted both hands and included the stress fractures, so it was hard to imagine how he designed and crafted the things he did. Like those fancy adjustable stilts in the shape of lightning bolts and spray-painted metallic gold, which Priest would strap on, sometimes with his pj's on under his parka, and suddenly there he'd be, staring down at us through the opaque plastic. Like he was eight feet tall, both hands holding onto the flat roof edge, a blurry silhouette, and the last of the daylight vanishing behind him.

It was at times like that when I'd glimpse how another man's kid might grow on you over time, though time, of course, was finally what took its toll in an outpost as long wintered and desolate as ours. Population just under fourteen hundred, a boomtown that never did, as my old man liked to say, and where even the richest among us was at least another half-dozen lifetimes away from banking that first million, and the next actual town with bowling alleys and movie theaters and without its name painted across the water tower was almost sixty miles distant.

Nonetheless, Priest clearly liked where he was. Liked school and farting around in the woodshop, half of which had doubled as Calcheck's gym before he took down and rolled up all the fight posters: Marciano, Dempsey, and, his all-time *numero uno*, Jake LaMotta, the Raging Bull. I helped pile the free weights, push aside the barbells and bench into a far corner. The stationary bike and skip ropes and footlocker. "No más," he said. "Enough." We clinked bottles to that, and to all those squat thrusts and two hundred sit-ups per workout, the before daylight five-mile runs.

And so far no change of heart, no talk about coming out of retirement. The only remnant of that life was the red, sweat-stained, heavy leather bag that still hung from a back rafter. Sometimes Priest would shorten his stilts and walk close up and flail away while Calcheck bandsawed and planed and belt-sanded on whatever project he'd been commissioned to do, sometimes from as far south as Alpena or Grand Rapids. He'd deliver anywhere in the state, and, should he be forced to spend the night in a Microtel or a Motel 6, he'd never fail to call home with an update, ask if everyone was doing okay.

As for the dad thing? Never married and kid-free his entire life, he didn't miss a beat. Took to it like magic, like he'd welcome every fatherless child out there into the fold. We're talking the epitome of patience, unguarded and upbeat and soft-spoken. Watchful. Doted on the kid. Come Priest's bedtime, it was Calcheck who'd leave the kitchen table and read to him, books from the library that they'd checked out together. It was Calcheck who made breakfast and waited with him each morning for the school bus while Sherri-Lynn slept in or slept it off, then mooned around until noontime, her brain a fog that finally lifted after that fourth or fifth cup of black coffee. "Who'd have thought," I said to her one time. "Of all people, look who's the softy underneath." Not meaning to make a comparison or imply that it was about time for her to upgrade *her* parenting skills. But all she offered back was this vacant, devaluating stare, as if the fantasy or temptation of something else had already raised its ugly head.

Her full name? Sherri-Lynn Jaxon with an *x*. The very first time I saw her waitressing, saw her legs, I thought, *Heat-seeking.* I thought, *Zero to sixty*, and hoped that Calcheck was riding it hard because this was a woman likely to blow through in a hurry: thin-shouldered and with oversize eyes that sometimes appeared silver, her coppery hair pulled back in a ponytail, a pale blue vein by her left temple. *Pretty*, I thought, *and not so pretty*, as in one day, Roller Derby, the next, *Dancing with the Stars.*

Plus she looked a lot of ages, depending on her mood and the angle and brightness of the light. Older than us whenever a match flame flickered across her face. But then, like a teenager, she'd hook her bare heels on the chair edge and tilt her head back and blow smoke rings toward the ceiling while the three of us drank beer in the kitchen and played this game she liked. A kind of make-it-up-as-you-go Trivial Pursuit, which, nine times out of ten, she won with the best questions *and* the best answers: Why does the skunk fear the owl? Answer: The owl has no sense of smell. Or, the follow-up: Okay, good, but double or nothing. Why then does the skunk fear the coyote? Answer: Simple, because, deep down like most of us, the coyote doesn't give a shit, and maybe even relishes the rankness. One brain-burner after the next, and each time she'd smile this smile I liked, and I'd concede that maybe she'd bucked over the ruts okay after all, and that landing in the boonies might actually constitute a more permanent commitment on her part. Maybe she was someone, as Calcheck liked to joke, who'd still be around to help lower you onto the throne in your old age.

She'd arrived in a Ford Festiva, which had recently given up the ghost and now sat rusting on blocks out back. Whatever her past, checkered or otherwise, not a whole lot of it had been revealed to me. Like she'd conveniently drawn blanks on long expanses of her own history, devoid of details and dates and anecdotes. Originally from Thunder Bay—or so she claimed—she'd married young. I bought that much, and the way she'd described her ex-husband the one time he got mentioned? A slug. A deadbeat son of a bitch whose clutches she'd finally escaped when she was nineteen and freebasing and suddenly on the run.

Along the way she'd ridden in a glass elevator in a city somewhere. Minneapolis maybe, Chicago, though I wondered if that translated better into dancing in a thong and six-inch heels under a rotating mirror ball, or diving half-naked for silver dollars in a mermaid tank. She was a woman who, after you'd had a drink or two, was easy enough to imagine straddling your lap with a scissor lock, or worse—inhabiting those recurring, wrong-minded midwinter dreams, where you'd try to flee on foot through snowdrifts up to your elbows, and the temperature at minus thirty-five degrees.

Didn't matter. In the here and now *as is* seemed good enough for Calcheck, and, our lives being what they were, that was plenty good enough for me as well.

CERTAIN EVENINGS after Sherri-Lynn left for work, Calcheck—as if drilling Priest on vocabulary words or multiplication tables—would say, "Repeat after me." Same exact routine, headings, and subheadings: home address and zip code, phone number, 911, the words and numerals that might someday save him or someone he loved. "If ever there's an emergency, or if you're scared or in trouble, you find a way and you call me and I'll come get you wherever you are. And if you can't reach me, you immediately try Uncle Oden's cell, okay?" It was an unlisted number, and Priest would rattle it off, too.

"His tin can and a string," Priest would say and giggle at how Calcheck had once described wireless. Living out on the fringes he wasn't far wrong, though rumor had it that a tower closer by was in the works, and the contract I'd taken out was half the price of a landline.

"And what else?" Calcheck said.

"That I remember every detail I can. I draw a picture in my head."

"Right, a mental map. Take in everything you can. Names of towns or businesses if you can sound them out. Billboards. Landmarks of any kind."

"Like Pictured Rocks or the world's biggest pie tin," Priest said, reaching for examples that Calcheck had described early on.

"Atta boy. But bottom line, and as soon as you can, you get to a pay phone and call home. Now, show me the quarter." And Priest would take it out of his pocket like a good luck charm and pantomime lifting the receiver and dropping the coin into the slot and dialing zero and reversing the charges, simple as that. "The operator," Calcheck said, "she'll take care of the rest, no questions asked."

"Why not tattoo the deal backward onto his bum?" I said. "And give him a hand mirror. Christ Almighty. Talk about overkill." But no call had yet come through, not from Priest or from Sherri-Lynn, and ever since their disappearance I'd dispensed with the wisecracking.

WE STILL HADN'T COME BACK AROUND to joking or laughing much, but I considered it a positive sign that the intricate scrollwork on the coffin's lid occupied Calcheck's mind enough to concentrate his attention. High-grade mahogany, and the contract timeline inexact, but like I told him, thirty days from diagnosis to the grave was how it went for my old man.

"Huh. Imagine that," was pretty much all he said after the diagnosis. Flat broke and no life insurance and barely time enough to put his affairs in order before going down for the count, liver cancer at fifty-one. Way before his time and mine, too. I was seventeen, and instead of renting a storage unit like I suggested, I hauled the entire contents of the house out onto the overgrown front lawn. An estate sale, as my stepmom called it—and she accepted every measly, cheapskate offer that came our way. What didn't sell got boxed up and donated to Goodwill.

To her credit, she stuck around just long enough to see me blunder along until graduation, at which point she drove away alone from our low-end modular where we lived those final days together before the impending foreclosure and eviction.

"Here, to tide you over," she said, and handed me sixty dollars, a wrinkled wad of ones and fives paper-clipped together, like she was trying to bribe or buy me off. And then she stared heavenward, as if into the cathedral ceiling she'd always dreamed about, talked about. "It just kills me," she said, "how a person plans ahead and again some more, a week from next Sunday or next year, and then, kerflooey. It ends like this, stranded in the damn breakdown lane."

I didn't weigh in on that, but truth be told my old man was a stickler about keeping his cars tuned and the oil changed, and good tread on the tires, emergency flares and a pair of jumpers in the trunk. Meaning that she packed off just fine to wherever she was headed, and I straightaway started in at the mill and survived most of that first summer in a tent at a campground, upwind of the showers and shitters, and biked to work each morning and back, no matter the weather. Some mornings I arrived soaked to the bone, my sneakers squeaking with every next step.

And from there, after two months of minimum-wage paychecks, I moved into a fully furnished one bedroom with a dinky two-burner stovetop, which allowed me to bank away money enough to open up a few options moving forward, whatever they might be. Night school somewhere for starters. Philosophy. Or possibly literature, given my interest in westerns and mystery novels, and how, when it came to similes and subject-verb agreement, I'd been an absolute wiz. "Experience the world and write about it, Oden," my tenth-grade English teacher Mrs. McKenzie once said to me. But already in my midthirties I'd still never ventured outside of the upper Midwest, and on certain endless late afternoons while working OT, lost in thought, I'd come to my senses. Like I'd been hallucinating, and I'd conclude that the wiser, more prudent plan was simply to abandon all ambition and stay put and, in another twenty years, retire early to Mexico, where I'd live like King Midas with his golden touch.

I never knew my birth mother, never badmouthed my step, though in defiance of advice I didn't need or want I've continued to this day to toast my old man, flipping each twist-off with my thumbnail, like a coin that comes up heads time after time after time.

And because I was stir crazy and bored and in the mood for some Waylon Jennings and Patsy Cline, a game or two of eight-ball, but mostly because I believed that it might do Calcheck a world of good to get out of the house and sip a few cold ones late on a Saturday night, I drove over and double honked to let him know it was me before I walked blind into the woodshop.

He was bent over, hands rock-steady and holding his diamond-tipped rotor. "Holy shit," I said. "I mean, rest in peace, I'm all about it, but Christ on a bike." And I brushed my fingertips across the intricately carved fangs, the curled-back lips, the intense, narrow-eyed stares of hyenas and timber wolves and wolverines and jackals—a pack of angry gods or devils.

"No angel wings or harps?" I said, and he said back, "Not so much, but listen to this." And his knuckles tap-tapping the coffin lid sounded to me like the reverberating heartbeats of grieving wild animals.

"And somebody actually ordered this?" I said, but Calcheck just shrugged, like, hey, you got demons to keep at bay, *you* decide who or what you want standing guard at the gate.

I took that to mean each to his own, my sentiments exactly, and I said as much. But eternity still seemed like a reach from where we were standing, a serious downer, and what I conjured instead was a chance encounter with a certain woman whose belt loops I might slide my thumbs through and who I might slow-dance with deep into the night. Sometimes she'd wear this soft lavender-colored sweater, the kind of fabric you might slide over an expensive flute or violin. If the stars aligned just so, I might escort her home from Bootleggers, a local watering hole out on Route 35 that we frequented now and again, though it'd been a while since we'd last closed it down.

Calcheck looked beaten up, his eyes puffy and red-rimmed, and I said, "You 'bout ready for a break? You up for that? The beers are on me."

He checked his watch and then glanced at the wall phone, his disfigured face unshaven, and under the low-hanging fluorescent lights I could see way more gray than I'd ever noticed. Like he'd aged ten years over the last week and a half. I figured that he hadn't slept much, if at all, and that he'd beg off on the offer. To convince him otherwise, I almost said that wherever Sherri-Lynn had stolen away to wouldn't be solved by hanging out with an empty coffin full of ghost tunes, regardless of the urgency and the price tag. That tomorrow would roll back at us soon enough, and that eventually she'd trip up and fall hard, and that we'd get wind of it whenever she did, one way or another, and we'd track her down and go from there. But in the meantime, I'd brought along a roll of quarters for the jukebox, and no disrespect to the dying, but since when did *we* lie down and roll over?

I could hear snow ticking the metal roof and the wind picking up, and maybe because we used to like running the roads on nights like that, Calcheck said, "Come on, let's hit it," and he grabbed his jacket and a pack of smokes. I thought, *Okay*, and in my best Rocky Balboa, I bobbed and weaved my way to and out the door, my truck at high idle and the headlights walleyed, punch-drunk more like, as if stunned and cutting two split-tailed tunnels into the darkness.

WE'D BOTH KNOCKED BACK a couple quick shots of Fireball. Doubles for Calcheck and more likely than not on an empty stomach. I'd seen it before and figured worst case at this pace he'd wake up come daybreak possessed of the serious shakes and shivers. But so far no double vision — at least not for me — and our reflections in the mirror more or less resembled us, and so I lowered my beer and said, "Hey, don't look now, but unless I'm mistaken, our happy hunters from yesterday morning just walked in."

"That a fact?" Calcheck said.

"Got a fair idea," I said, and he nodded and turned sideways on his stool, chin tucked into his shoulder.

"Fancy that," he said. "And standing just like we left them, fat assed and pissed off and cold."

They were wearing vests and hadn't moved from in front of the entryway, the joint half-empty. Mounted above the last tier of tightly stacked bottles behind the bar was a trophy ten-point whitetail, Christmas balls hanging from each tine, a red bow fastened around its neck. The buck seemed to be grinning, as if he might wink down at us with one of those bulging, glassy black eyeballs.

"Anywhere you like," the bartender called over. "Be right with you."

We'd been there just short of an hour and I said, "Finish up?" Calcheck shook his head to being chased away a second time, and he signaled for another round. They seemed not to have noticed us yet, and possibly they wouldn't if they slid into one of those high-backed booths, though even after they did I wasn't convinced that Calcheck didn't intend one way or another to take this whole thing outside. "Blue Bayou" was playing, and Lee-Anne Mazzocco, the woman I'd hoped might show, hadn't yet, though I'd been watching for her in the mirror every time that front door jangled.

"Hold the fort," Calcheck said, and spun left toward the men's room. He wasn't gone thirty seconds when I felt the cellphone's murmur in my pocket. No one ever called at that hour, and the name that came up I didn't recognize. Normally I wouldn't have answered—a crank or misdial—but just in case I said, "Hello," and walked the call out into the parking lot, where it was still snowing, the connection mostly scratch and static, but when I said, "Priest, is that you?" a voice answered, "Yes." It sounded far away.

"Can you hear me? Are you okay?" I asked, every other word of his in delayed reaction, a whisper just out of earshot. "I can't hear you. Is it safe for you to talk louder? Can you do that? You're breaking up."

I heard "nobody" and "alone" and "locked," and I covered my left ear and angled away from the noise of an idling eighteen-wheeler.

"Men," he said, and faded out again, and I said, "How many?" and a few seconds later he said, "No, two e's . . . at the end," and I said, "You mean Menominee?" I took a few more steps toward the highway, and he said, "Please." He was crying.

"Where in Menominee? Where, Priest? Just tell me that," and when I repeated the name I thought he said, the line went dead. "You there? Priest?"

"Don't bother," someone just beyond my peripheral vision said. "The service around here sucks big-time."

I doubted he meant the phone or the bar, but I recognized the voice right off, and I said, "Depends on the night, I guess."

"Or who shows up to ruin it. To fuck up the party. You boys got a real knack for that."

That same alpha-male bullshit, and definitely no kill tags punched out, and a growing vendetta to avenge. When he unzipped his vest and handed it to his silent hunting buddy, I said, "Hey, sorry about yesterday. Bad timing on our part, but I've got somewhere I need to get to right now. Maybe we can finish this another time."

"Now's good," Calcheck said, and stepped between us, like he'd appeared out of nowhere, an apparition who'd floated down from the sky, both hands in his coat pockets. "If it's payback you're after, let's get this done and over with, yeah?"

The guy nodded and smiled and shuffle-stepped forward, his sucker punch telegraphed and so slow that Calcheck ducked it and shrugged before he unloaded with that lethal trademark left hook of his, a single punishing blow just under the ribcage. It was over that fast, the guy on his knees, doubled up and hugging himself and moaning like he'd been gutshot. He kept gasping and gulping for air. Said, "Oh," and then again, his head pitched forward, and I thought for sure he'd start coughing up blood in the snow.

"What's *your* name?" Calcheck said, and the tagalong cleared his throat and answered, "Garnette Stokes," and Calcheck said, "Well, Garnette, how about you step right over here and help us lift him up. Back seat or bed?" Garnette pointed to a pickup and said, "That's my truck over there, the Silverado," and it took all three of us to load that bulk onto his back, where he curled up and kept moaning. Calcheck leaned over the side and said, "Back in the day," but he didn't finish, and turned instead and said to Garnette, "Someone should've clocked him a long time ago. Drape something over him and get him back to wherever you're staying. And tomorrow go home."

I'd never been in a fistfight. Not even a serious shoving match, though I'd sparred one time with Calcheck, three two-minute rounds on a timer, just to experience what mortal combat might feel like. I wore headgear and a mouthpiece and a cup, a kidney belt, and when Calcheck smiled and offered to tie one hand behind his back, I said, "Bullshit." I said, "Come on, bring it. You're mine, motherfucker," and called him a patsy, a cherry. We touched gloves like it was on for real, the adrenalin pumping harder every time I let my hands go, though nothing solid landed.

He flicked out a few stiff jabs, an occasional straight right without a whole lot behind it, but shifted to southpaw and finished the final round with a three-punch flurry that stung and momentarily made my lips go numb. A scrape on the bridge of my nose, some redness, but otherwise I walked away pretty much unmarked. "That all you got?" I said, and he nodded, called it a draw, and we took off the gloves and drank to that, too.

But there in the parking lot I understood how a man inclined by instinct and circumstance and skill—a trained fighter, even one beyond his prime, could, anytime he wanted, hurt another man at will. And Calcheck had, yet the spectacle in no way constituted a victory. Furthermore, it settled nothing. As my old man used to say, "Oden, walk away. No one ever wins, regardless the outcome," and I could see that clear as day on Calcheck's face.

We watched the pickup's taillights fade, and from somewhere there was the distant whine of a snowmobile.

Everyone on the move, and I hoped that wherever we were headed next would not end ugly or violent, worse than what had already occurred. The gas tank was almost full, and the county plows would be out soon, and I said, "Priest called. We can find him, I think, if that's still what you want to do. I'll go pay for the drinks and be right back."

I KILLED THE HEADLIGHTS and the engine, and we coasted right up in front of number five, the end unit in a U-shape of cabins, all of them identical and rundown, a single canopied halogen on a light pole. Not that Priest had provided me with such details, but the busted-up

Monte Carlo four-door best fit the description I'd concocted in my mind: worn out and the ass end low-slung, as if half a foot of light, dry November powder had flattened the suspension.

We'd driven almost four hours. The lighted sign said VACANCY, but the office windows were dark. It could be that we'd missed Priest and Sherri-Lynn by minutes or seconds—right place, wrong time—or just as likely wrong all the way around, though neither of us appeared alert enough to see past the fact of where we were parked: On the edge of the world, as I saw it, and, as if it were fated, all we needed to do was toot the horn and Priest would emerge, all packed and ready to go. Like a shared custody agreement had been drawn up, and there we were, right on time as always.

In other words, we *had* no plan, but we had long passed the point of no return, and I wondered if we'd simply sit tight until the door opened and someone stepped into view. Possibly total strangers, oblivious to any threat or rescue, a family on their way somewhere who had nothing whatsoever to do with us other than a hurried, piecemeal conversation that in all likelihood I'd deciphered incorrectly. I lit a cigarette and let a few more minutes pass before I said, "I'll take the first watch. You get some sleep."

Calcheck had been flexing his left wrist off and on, as if he'd busted something, and his eyes, when he looked over at me, were mere slits. He'd taken a serious pounding, entirely overmatched like most of us when it comes to love, if that's what it was, its terms and considerations, none of them binding or legal and, in that regard, the outcome already known. We had no rights in the matter. Kidnappers—that's who we'd be, harshly judged in the icy silence of first light if Calcheck *did* step out of the truck and knock on or force open or negotiate through the locked cabin door. Whatever was holding him upright in his seat, I hadn't the foggiest.

All I remember was that I slouched down, and hours later I woke shivering, a dusting of snow on the windshield, and Calcheck gone.

Like I'd driven home from the bar after dropping him off and passed out behind the wheel in my own driveway.

I hit the wipers, a single swipe, and not ten feet in front me was this sack of bones of a creature, arms crossed, fingers massaging his skinny biceps. Like some cartoon figure, black hair slicked back, wearing a T-shirt and pointy black shoes but no socks, hopping from one foot to the other. Every few seconds he'd squint back at the cabin window, his lips chapped and raw, and when finally he caught a glimpse of me behind the windshield, he froze.

I tried to quick-shake the cobwebs, everything strange and spooky-quiet like the set of a silent movie, like a dream. I tried to insert myself into the dialogue I imagined going on inside and hoped that Sherri-Lynn was alert enough to listen to reason. That her kid was headed for foster care and that she was on a fast track into rehab or prison. If she had no interest in saving herself, at least she might agree to let Priest finish the school year and see what the world looked like then. Or better yet, she might just walk out with him, her hair blond again like when she'd first arrived and we'd all sat together for the first time in Calcheck's kitchen.

But only Priest stepped out and waved to me, and I started the engine and leaned over and pushed open the passenger-side door. He seemed okay.

"Are you okay?" I said, and he nodded. "Just tired. And hungry." Calcheck followed a few minutes later, the speed freak all wound up again and dancing his deranged jig in the snow. I hoped Calcheck wouldn't coldcock him, and he didn't. He slid into the cab and said, "Go," though he fixed on the cabin window as if the drapes might part.

I looked, too, though all I could see was the reflection of the truck getting smaller and smaller as it reversed out of the lot. And the clouds parting just enough for that first glimpse of blue, and Priest already asleep between us.

THE ALCHEMIST'S APPRENTICE

For Vince Gilligan

MY MOM SAYS she hasn't the foggiest and that wherever Jimmy Creedy, her stay-over boyfriend, heisted all those tracheotomy tubes is anybody's guess. "Possibly Dr. Frankenstein's la-bor-a-tory," I joked, but she just shrugged, like yeah, maybe.

For everyone's sake she asks Jimmy no questions, and neither do I. The less *we* know the better, and it's been a few months since he liquefied the pure-grade silver and poured it into cookie molds right there on our kitchen counter. Untraceable angels and mermaids and dog bones and bells. Then he double-boxed and packed them like bullion, and sometime after midnight he returned, saying, "Mm-hmm," and my mom in her nightgown sashaying toward him, and Jimmy already toasting to "rubies on the mud-flaps. Goddamn stardust instead of brake lights."

That's the way he talks, always high as a kite after a lucrative score, everything in code, and I figured what he meant was that we were all three of us together suddenly headed for happier times.

A godsend is what my mom contends, given our circumstances. He's late thirties like her and handsome as Han Solo — broad-cut across the chest but otherwise angular and tall and blue-eyed. Easygoing and good-humored, a state of mind that'd been all but snuffed out in our household. He's smart, too, and in ways you might not anticipate. Just last week he brainstormed some weird wind physics, inversions and updrafts and crosscurrents, which I then mapped and calibrated and reconstructed for my ninth-grade science project. An octagon of box fans arranged around a dunce stool so that when I hit the power switch the iridescent drawstrings of Evelyn Sacksteder's sweatshirt lifted slow-motion sideways and writhed and writhed like skinny, green electric eels in the darkened classroom.

A few girls shrieked, and later Evelyn whispered in my ear, "Alchemist." She whispered, "Sorcerer," but it's Jimmy Creedy who possesses the magic, the Midas touch, not me. Just last week I opened the door as he unhooked my mom's bra and somehow pulled it through the sleeve of her T-shirt. He grinned and winked over her shoulder at me as if someday, against impossible odds, I, too, might perform such wizardry.

Plus he's the one who got my mom to brush back all that heavy dark hair from her forehead and face, and when they slow dance in the kitchen those oxidized metal earrings he polished now glow bright as mercury under the low-wattage light bulbs. If she tilts her head just so, that shapeless, wicked-purple skin graft covering her entire left cheek appears almost soft. He kisses her there like she's still pretty, like this is her most gorgeous feature, though she's so afraid of fire that she stood back, palms out, and stared through her splayed fingers when that whispery blue whoosh of my Bunsen burner ignited.

I guess having lighted it makes me an accessory or accomplice. And later, when Jimmy licked his thumb, peeled some bills from his money clip, and handed me a couple of freshly minted twenties, I nodded and wadded them up like he said so they didn't look so new, and then I stuffed, one each, deep into my front pockets.

Ever since the attack my mom's been out of work; the manager at Kroger's not saying so, but what he meant was that no amount of makeup and cover-stick could alter the sight of her in the customers' eyes. Worst of all my mom said it made her feel like a tramp, all painted up and begging like that, though prior to Jimmy's arrival she'd continued to religiously circle in red magic marker every possible lead in the want ads. She even checked the Laundromat bulletin board, and I racked *my* brain for any conceivable scheme to generate some income. Each time she left she'd say, "Wish me luck," but it'd be the predictable once-over-and-gone as soon as she showed up in person.

"God help us, Rollo," she'd say after each interview, the gauze removed, and what she described as live wasps chewing and chewing underneath those blisters. Her right eyebrow was singed permanently bald, and she's got a fake one that makes her look extraterrestrial on that side. And no health insurance or emergency strongbox buried in our backyard. No savings whatsoever to advance the prospects of any additional surgery, the doctors polite and well wishing and already rolling in dough, not one of them saying, "Okay, pay what you can and we'll continue forward."

Deeve's the one responsible for the disfigurement, a gas canister strapped to his back and the flame waves warping skyward from the homemade blowtorch every time he squeezed the trigger. He's a roofer by trade, but this had nothing to do with shingles or eves or melting tar, the gypsy moths everywhere — translucent, balled-up, swarming greenish-black tents of them. I'd long ago dubbed him Evil Deeve, which my mom didn't like, but when we pulled into the gravel driveway that evening, half the trees on our property were already ashed out. Even the higher branches of the chokecherries, the leaves heat-torn and wilted, and the bark on the birches like parchment, still sparking alive and dying.

A self-appointed exterminator from hell was my take, coveralls and outsized gloves and goggles but no hat. The orange flare of the sun reflected off the windows, as if he'd torched the house, too, intending to burn it right to the ground. Each oily blast lasted maybe ten seconds is all, oblong and up-rushing, and after each one my mom barely able to catch her breath, as if all the oxygen was being sucked out of the cab.

"What has he done?" she said. "Where did he get that?" and I said back, "Let's get out of here, Mom," the loud p-shush of each fire cloud like distant bomb bursts.

She shifted into park and powered up the windows and said, "You stay put. Stay right here." Then she exited, the engine idling, and her skirt off-white and tight fitting as she walked toward him, that bangle on her skinny ankle catching the low light and her ponytail swaying from side to side. Deeve's back was to us, shoulders hunched, and the low-slung metal lawn chair, where my mom liked to sit and read in the shade, was upended, the paint peeled and twisted.

A user and a scrounge—that's what he is. A freeloader, straight up lazy, a bully, a serious Section 8 if you ask me. Why my mom allowed him to stay around remains a mystery and a curse. Especially after he'd go Jekyll-Hyde and, absent any warning, say, "The fuck you say what? You smart-mouthed little bastard, I'll clock you so bad it'll make your piss turn purple. You hear me?"

Yes or no it didn't matter. First word out he'd turn slaphappy, backhanding me upside the head for what any reasonable adult would deem your normal, healthy, everyday kid-type talkback. Nothing close-fisted or knockdown, but enough to hurt, and my mom yelling, "Stop it. Leave him alone, goddamn you. As God is my witness don't you ever lift a hand to my son." And from me, not another peep, though I was wishing, for all the world, that my dad would appear out of thin air and stomp Deeve half-dead with his size thirteens. Those exact same combat boots that he'd worn home, not from any war but rather from two hours northbound of here, where he'd been stationed at Camp Grayling, and where he'd washed out for insubordination. Dustups, as he called them, dead-end and schoolyard stupid, but, like he said, once you take sides against someone or something, make it matter. Make it stick. And my mom screaming, "Get out or so help me. You're all done here. Nothing but trouble and more trouble right from the start," and Evil Deeve slamming his way gone, only to pussy back the next day, all hangdog and choked-up with pathetic promises and apologies. "You'll see," he'd say. "Please. I messed up, but I swear it'll never happen again. We'll work this through," a drill they perfected, and for long stretches he'd seem to her like a penitent and decent man, what she called the demons long-fought and possibly, this time, conquered.

"Fat chance," I'd say. "He's whacko, Mom, he's deep-down mean-minded, right to the core. Don't you trust him, not one iota," but she'd cave, as usual, saying, "Give him one more chance, Rollo." Always one more, and now there he was, crazed and waging war as if we'd been invaded by a gazillion tiny vipers or black widows—our backyard nuked-out—and the fire whorls blasting and boomeranging randomly everywhere around him. No neighbors and so no sirens, and I thought to grab the hose and douse the house and the low, slant-roofed out-building. But she looked back right then and pointed at me to stay put, stay out of this, that she'd handle him same as always.

I could smell the burning larva stench, and the standing corn in the field beyond him was golden-cloaked in the dying sunlight, and before I could shout out or hit the horn, that slow-motion sweep of fire was already on her. She did not scream or pass out or go up in flames or even pirouette away. And Deeve, staring beyond her at me, as if unaware of why I was running full-tilt toward where he stood above that slight depression, the grass there still deep green, and my mom on her knees, head lowered, and hugging herself and shivering.

IT WAS RULED AN ACCIDENT. No priors, no history of arson or assault, and his "Vote Satan" bumper sticker not so much telltale as it was, according to the judge, Deeve's First Amendment right. I expected as much on account of how my dad used to say to me whenever *he'd* gotten a raw deal, "What law?" Still, if the punishment fit the crime, I maybe wouldn't sentence Deeve to the electric chair, but an extended stretch in solitary confinement is the least he deserved for first-degree carelessness and permanent cruel hurting. There's an injunction against him ever setting foot on the premises again, and on the off chance that he someday circles back from wherever he's at, Jimmy Creedy says a little abracadabra and, poof, nothing left of the linger-ing rank stench of that bottom dweller and his cheap ass aftershave.

Knocking around is where Jimmy's from. "Here, there," he maintains. Meaning no port of entry and no previous or forwarding address. At least not one he intends to divulge. And, if he's telling it straight, not fifteen seconds of his former life spent in juvie or Jackson or anywhere else in these continental United States. Not that he hasn't dodged a bullet or two, but as far as he knows his mug hasn't appeared on anyone's most wanted. Nor has anyone picked him out of a lineup, and whatever it takes he aims to keep it that way.

He claims if necessary he can turn as invisible as wind, and his physical presence in the house is pretty minimal. My mom has cleared a narrow space in her closet for him, but from what I've observed Jimmy hasn't, in all this time, unpacked much beyond some toiletries and a change of clothes from his van. Unlike me he never raids the fridge or answers the telephone, not that it rings off the hook or anything close to that. He takes navy showers and wipes down the tiles and the floor. Sometimes he'll walk outside and just stand there, as if approximating some impossible-to-gauge distance. It could be that the countdown has already begun, though he hasn't, and to my mom's liking, actually mentioned any immediate departure plans.

Plus he pays rent. An allotment I'd call beyond generous even though he oftentimes goes missing for two or three nights running. We never know where to, but no matter when or how late he arrives back, he'll tiptoe into my bedroom, gently shake my shoulder, and whisper, "Rollo, get dressed," which I always do, and then I go help him unload the merchandise. Each time we finish he slow-nods and slips me quadruple what my mom on those slow rotating shifts used to take home in tips when she waitressed weekends at Aladdin's Lamp and Lounge out on Route 28. What Jimmy calls walking-around money, the outbuilding his stockroom now, the worthless debris that Deeve pack-ratted away long carted off to the county dump, the 2x4 wood stob replaced by a serious combination padlock you couldn't hacksaw off if you spent all day trying. And that solitary window boarded over.

My mom never ventures out there—to King Tut's tomb, as I secretly dubbed it. I haven't mentioned word one about what's out there. No exceptions, and so she couldn't, if interrogated, implicate anyone or identify any of the inventory, the brass candelabras and those sterling silver half-pint flasks with the ornate engravings of fish and pheasants and large-headed water dogs. Plus my favorite by far, a set of six Chinese throwing stars, which, if I smuggled them into school, would bring me half a fortune. And sidearming a couple into Bry Randell and Jake Payette's metal lockers would shut those half-wits up right now and forever.

But nothing sits around for very long. The way in is the way out, as Jimmy says, import/export, good morning and goodnight. As far as I can determine he operates solo. I've never admitted it, but I wouldn't mind partnering with him some night and maybe up the pay grade enough to get my mom's surgery underway before the snow flies. I've socked away every coppery red cent I've made so far, but the fact of the matter is that without Jimmy it'll require another half-dozen lifetimes.

I can tell my mom's nervous that sooner or later she'll wake up or look up from her book or magazine and find Jimmy vanished, as if he never actually existed, a vision or genie or guardian angel she merely daydreamed into being. In perfect reverse of how he first appeared, his van nosed sideways to our front door, and him leaning out his window like he'd just pulled up to a drive thru for some iced tea and a corn dog. I remember how she stepped outside—legs shaved and her hair still shiny and wet from the shower—onto the narrow porch right beside me in full afternoon daylight, her hands on her hips. Skirt and flip-flops but no lipstick and without those oversize, maroon-framed sunglasses to face, close up, whoever this intruder or gawker happened to be, him tipping his baseball cap and never once wincing or gaping away and instead saying, "Hello. Excuse me. Sorry to bother." Saying, "Ma'am."

And then all three of us trekking out toward my dad's Corvair Monza Spyder, where, in the late evenings, my dad would sit and chain-smoke Pall Malls and drink up to a twelve-pack of Black Label while he listened to the Detroit Tigers on the radio. Click down that row of square plastic buttons—didn't matter which one—and what you got was Ernie Harwell, as if all stations led here, to our box seat of a car. No wheels and up on cinder blocks and the windshield pitted and BB cracked, but the play-by-play so clear most nights you could almost hear those home run blasts sizzle and rise like you were there live at the ballpark. He'd had in mind to cherry the car out one unaffordable used part at a time, right down to the brake shoes and pin stripes, using a chamois to buff the hubcaps and the chrome grill into a high-blinding glitter. Sometimes he'd even pitch forward over the steering wheel, check the side-view mirror, and quick-hit the turn signal, then double-clutch as if we were about to pull out and pass our own nowhere lives right here on the outskirts of this nowhere town.

He'd say, "All goes according to plan, and by your sixteenth birthday . . ." but more and more that thin, hollow drop in his voice, the silent nod, which wasn't at all like him. Already it's been five years since the diagnosis. Cancer of the pancreas, my dad dead and buried within five weeks and me still a full year shy of my driver's permit.

"Whoo-ee. Check *this* out," Jimmy Creedy said. "The genuine article." And then he referred to the Corvair as a classic, as if just saying so might transform some backyard trash heap into that far-flung image my dad had of it. But like Jimmy later said to me, sometimes love at first sight requires a higher power the closer you get. And when he jerked open the driver's side door and looked inside, he just shrugged the deal dead, the red vinyl upholstery worn and torn open and the floor reinforced with two squares of warped fiberboard. Plus that free-fall pyramid of my dad's empties on the back seat, the ashtray grubby and humped up with decomposing cigarette butts.

Not that there'd been a For Sale sign posted or any dickering, though we sure could have used whatever he might have offered, even the favor of towing it away. The place was already junked up enough. My mom, in tears, once said to me, "We'll be fine, Rollo," which I knew to be untrue when she added, a poor choice of phrase, "If only I could walk out of this body." She meant above the breastbone. Below there she's shapely and thin, and from a distance she can still cast a trance on most any man. But close that distance and they spear on past.

"May I?" Jimmy said, right out of the blue, like he was asking her to dance. And before she could answer he was holding her fingers and turning her hand slowly over and back as he checked out every tiny charm on her braceleted wrist. Unicorn and sea horse and leprechaun, a cloverleaf and a miniature pewter comb and hand mirror—one of the few pieces of jewelry she still owned and, like a schoolgirl, had started wearing again. She'd pawned the rest for next to nothing, for tub fare, as she said, and she was crying when she pulled out that fancy bottle of honey-almond bath oil. Like some secret potion that might soothe the insides of her thighs, where all that living skin had been flayed and borrowed away, half her face bright purplish red and glassy as cling wrap, and her new eyelid seeming to droop another centimeter every other day.

A DREAM JOB it's probably not, graveyard and minimum wage to begin. No health bennies or incentive bonuses, but here's the thing: my mom says that it's a regular paycheck, time and a half on the weekends, and vacation days after the first full year's employment. Best of all the hours are hers alone. Minus those truckers, of course, who quip and flirt with her over the front gate intercom, their come-to-me voices scratchy and distant, and who transport everything from hindquarters to hog hearts and chicken parts. They pull in from places as foreign as El Paso, Texas, and Albuquerque, New Mexico, and then follow her directions through the grid of loading and unloading docks at Louie's Cold Storage, nicknamed the Morgue.

Princess, they call her. Honey-Heart and Ghost Girl, and they beg themselves upstairs or downstairs — "Wherever you're hiding, hold tight" — and they'll beeline it right to her front door. A steady windfall of late-night love offers and my mom with the desk lamp on lowest power and the office blinds drawn to the bottom of the window wells. I reasoned that if she let those guys see her, they'd maybe take up a collection in her name. But when I offered that as a possibility she made clear in no uncertain terms that some sad-sack charity case or pity prize she wasn't, and that precious little in this life could convince her otherwise. "Okay. All right, I'm sorry," I said, and she said back, "They're just a bunch of road-weary, lonely cowboys," and Jimmy with a sudden, deep drawl, wisecracking, "Yeah, all prod and no cattle." He's good like that, quick on the draw, all jostle and jibe and getting her to loosen up and laugh, no matter her mood. Sometimes he'll get extra-animated and grabby and tickle her until she begs him to stop.

He's the one who found the posting, and, first thing after my mom got hired, he pulled out two almost invisibly thin, gold-rimmed wine-glasses and poured them near to full. My mom's not much of a drinker, though maybe she should be, given how she turned giggly and played along when Jimmy requested, all serious like, that she provide him and me with a secret map to the frozen vaults of Walt Disney and Ted Williams. Which I at first didn't get, but after he explained it seemed no more farfetched than that movie I'd seen at the Victory Theater with my dad, where some ten-thousand-year-old iceman perfectly preserved blinks wide-awake under those scientists' giant thaw lights.

"A little too much Jesus in that," my dad said on the ride home. "I mean, turn that trick and who in the old neighborhood's still there waiting? We're talking about a corpse, for Christ's sake, picking up where it left off?"

I shrugged and said, "You never know, I guess," and concentrated more on the radio tower lights pulsing red way out ahead of us in the night sky, and my dad, per usual, drove way too fast, like we were being pursued by somebody or something. His thinking was always the same, that this life was this life, one and done, and gone for good. What you see is what you get, and, "Hoo boy, take a gander at what it's offered up for the likes of us. And what's more," he said, "let's assume I'm wrong and that you could come back. Well, all fine and good." But he concluded that even if you did, it'd be as some dung beetle or cutworm, and for damn sure not as yourself.

I glanced over at him, not liking when he'd get to talking like that, loose-tongued and saying stuff just to get *me* all riled up and angry, like he did way too much of the time. And to make things worse he'd just been terminated from another job, no severance pay, and my mom earlier that same evening tearing into him for what she called his pride and his asinine, jackass principles. "No, not convictions. Liabilities," she said, meaning his short fuse and forever running off at the mouth, though as often as not it was the combination of both their raised voices that pounded nonstop in my eardrums.

It wasn't until after my dad got sick that the house finally quieted. And, naturally, way more so during that final hospital vigil, where, a few seconds after the monitor's green blips suddenly flatlined, he woke from his coma and said, "Oh. God, no, not so soon." And my mom having already run out into and down the corridor, screaming for help. Before his eyes blinked and then blinked open again like tiny, distant fires, it seemed that possibly days or even lifetimes had passed. He'd aged tenfold, his lips bruised and his arm all boned-out white and skinny, the flesh almost translucent as he reached for me and whispered, "Don't keep back. Not now, Rollo," and when I stepped closer he confided in me his wish to be cremated, his ashes spread along our property line to boundary off any evil spirits. "Tell me that you'll see to it," he said. "Say it now." And I did. "I promise," I said, at the exact instant that my mom reentered with a nurse, followed by a doctor a couple minutes later, who failed to revive him and thumb-shut my dad's eyes, pronouncing him officially deceased.

The next day I pleaded and pleaded with my mom when, instead of an urn, she purchased a bargain package casket and headstone, assuring me that I'd momentarily entered the fits was all. "Shock," she said. "Fear and grief and delirium. It's not uncommon." And made, she insisted, all the more terrible by him dying so young. "On top of that, your father . . . he wasn't a pagan, he'd never talk like that. Like voodoo and spells and hexes. Like we were born under some bad omen or sign? Rollo, there's no accounting for how things happen as they do, but what you *thought* you heard, it's not remotely possible. The dead, they don't speak to us that way, out loud with real words. It's a figment of your imagination, okay? Listen to me, listen to what I'm saying." But I just shook my head, refusing to be reasoned out of what I knew outright to be actual and true.

"It happened exactly like I said. He talked to me while you went for help, and nothing will ever change that," I said, and to this day I'd swear to it on the Bible, whatever my mom or anyone else believes. Period. And when she pressed the back of her hand to my forehead I turned away, and her final words on the subject? "I should never, ever have left you alone in that room with him."

No wake, and so no ushers or pallbearers, the plain pine casket already suspended on a lift above the open grave when we arrived at the cemetery. And waiting graveside was some white-haired minister she'd hired for what felt to me like a four- or five-minute service, not a single word of which I heard. Otherwise, family members only, meaning my mom and me, and although she worried herself sick that I might suffer nightmares from the whole ordeal, none ensued. Not then they didn't, and not now, either. But before Jimmy Creedy I'd sometimes lie wide-awake half the night, lost in thought and believing that if my mom had only listened to me, that running tally of weirdos and losers who courted her would've fled the demons of my dad's ghost before they'd ever dared step foot inside our house.

ALL WEEK Jimmy's been picking me up from detention, as if by some unspoken agreement the responsibility has fallen to him. He always waits outside in his van, half a block away and on the opposite side of the street, like he's casing the joint in broad, late-afternoon daylight while I sit alone in the front row of the deserted classroom. My punishment? To reflect, as Vice-Principal Wazniak said, on what I'd done. He was, he said, in the face of all that had in the past months befallen us, sorry, but me acting out this way wouldn't benefit a thing. "You think about that," he said, and something about fitting in and possibly someday attending an accredited community college. As if on his say-so my future had, on the spot, been assigned. Like an extra credit essay on some dumb-butted subject like pride or perseverance in order to avoid a failing final grade. "Come on, a smart kid like you ought to step up," he said, in his standard, slow-motion monotone of doom, "and set a better example." That same old soul-suck, as Jimmy put it, which in his book merited all of about two shallow seconds' worth of serious contemplation.

Mid-November and fall already a distant memory. Heavier snow in the forecast and the last of those great honking, high-up V's of Canada geese winging somewhere way south of here, I'd form this mental image of Evelyn Sacksteder, her hair jet-black and sleek and tumbling past her shoulders. And wearing jeans so tight you'd have to lubricate a dime and press down hard in order to slide it even half an inch into either of those rear pockets.

It passed the time, though mostly what I thought about was my mom, who'd resorted to wearing a pirate patch, her puffy right eye just about completely closed. I'd seen her slowly lift the lid between her index finger and thumb to let in some light, and then she'd cover her other eye, attempting to silently read the tiny black print in the newspaper's classifieds. "Women seeking men," Jimmy interpreted aloud and winked over at me, though my mom's strange look made apparent that she found the joke unfunny. And even though her vision was still twenty-twenty, she worried nonetheless about going blind if the eyelid wasn't repaired soon. I thought then about those underground cave-dwelling fish I'd read about in *National Geographic*, their pupils a mottled murky white.

Needless to say, I left that part out when explaining the detention and admitted only to how the school librarian had spied me opening the scissors of my Swiss Army knife and cutting from the magazine's glossy pages the bamboo-punctured faces of half-naked women from some long-forgotten tribe in Zimbabwe. I'm not even sure *why* I did it, except perhaps to illustrate to my mom that beauty's in the eye of the beholder. Jimmy claims it is, but my mom's faith is in her bankbook, which has been looking fairly decent finally, thereby bettering, as she says, the prospects of her full return to genuine personhood.

This past weekend, while she was at work, I helped Jimmy extract the platinum from half a dozen mud-caked catalytic converters. It's the first time he's implicated me by association, confessing that he'd pilfered them from the underbellies of the county school buses. "Just returning the favor. Payback," he said, as if to raise the stakes on the petty thieving that *I'd* attempted and gotten busted for.

For whatever reason I flashed right then on my dad and the silver flecks of yet another worthless scratch ticket turning black under his thumbnail. Whenever he'd win back a small-change stake he'd immediately bet that away, too, saying that we were overdue—"You and me, Rollo"—as if being parked at the E-Z Mart marked the gateway into an easier, happier life. The odds dictated, he said, that sooner or later we'd hit a different turn, Lady Luck leveling our way for a change. Of course, she never did. Just ask my mom, who'd sum it up without a second's hesitation as that same insane, lingering-sad version of our earthly lives.

But enter Jimmy Creedy, who, as my mom gets to saying whenever he's away for more than a couple days, has both initiative and a plan, evidenced by that long-awaited initial surgery date finally marked with silver and red stars on our kitchen calendar. January 5 of the New Year.

A brand-new beginning and so go right ahead and count them off, only seven short weeks forthcoming. A miracle, she says, and in her book is it any wonder that she places Jimmy as someone who's been to the mountaintop and back?

She says that together we've almost done it, reached what we need to get started, but the truth is that it's Jimmy who's contributed the major portion. Me, I'm not even a junior partner, a beginning, beginning apprentice who keeps him company. And who on this night listens as he says, "Okay, hold 'em steady," referring to the empty lipstick canisters he slowly fills with thick oblong bubbles of liquid fire. "This here's the fun part," he says. "To make it new, fashioned and forged for a goddess."

That's what I marvel at most, how, right from the onset, he's envisioned my mom this way, and I can hardly wait for her to pick up and attempt to paint her lips with what she'll anticipate to be Peach Parfait or Eternal Rose.

I twist the caps back on and replace the tubes in a line of three on the back of her dresser top, like bullet-shaped bullion. I imagine them displayed behind glass in a museum, rather than in a deluxe double-wide out here in the middle of nowhere.

"Like turning straw into gold," I say, but he just shrugs, says, "Yeah." Says at least we're not wagging some battery-powered metal detector back and forth across the trail of our own lost and bewildered shadows.

He's smiling, but the tone sounds off, sounds sad and tired, and he says, "Hey. If the end result justifies the means," and I just nod and let it go at that.

UNTIL NOW Jimmy's never been gone for anywhere near this long, nine straight nights and days. But our standing rule of thumb: don't ask or speculate aloud. Still, my mom's been plenty worried and right before sunrise when she gets home, she'll pace in her slip from window to window, the world pitch dark outside.

Knock on wood she hasn't yet spiraled into shutdown mode as I've witnessed firsthand in the not-so-distant past. That's a positive sign, and yesterday she arrived home from the Morgue with a free holiday ham and half a dozen spicy, foot-long summer sausages. But hands down, her best early Christmas present to date, meaning ever, is the computerized mockup sketch of her new, as Dr. DiGregorio said, handing it to her, "Soon to be you." Complete with a red bow tied around the stand-up frame, like something for the mantle if only we'd had one. *Rejoice*, is what the taped-on gift card said, *in the spirit of this season*.

I'd probably have recognized her anyway, but the picture looked more like if she'd had a younger, long-out-of-touch sister, who, unannounced, showed up for the holidays at our front door. Higher cheekbones, fuller lips, and the skin's pigmentation nearly perfect.

A series of four procedures in the space of a year, the last with a medical tattoo specialist who guarantees to re-create, hair by individual hair, an all but foolproof eyebrow facsimile. A word, when my mom first pointed it out to me in the Explanation of Treatment, that I misread as *face smile*, as if, even in her deepest grief or outrage she'd never again appear anything other than content and young and beautiful.

But that's not how she appeared after discovering the lipstick tubes, frown lines deepening in her forehead, her hair uncombed. Like she'd put two and two together, and so no need to primp in anticipation of Jimmy showing up anytime soon. I'd played dumb on trouble stuff—mostly school related—plenty of times, but I'd never outright lied to her about important matters. But it felt like maybe I *had* been lying when she finally asked point blank whether Jimmy had mentioned anything to me about needing time alone, or if he seemed anxious or distracted or in a hurry. Different. Something on his mind that he'd opened up about? Something less *in*exact, she said, than all this guesswork and speculation? She talked about how unfair it was to leave someone hanging like this after so much time together. "Any sign, Rollo, that he might already be on his way elsewhere?"

What I wanted to say was that I liked but hardly knew him. A true statement of fact. And that maybe Jimmy Creedy wasn't even his real name, but instead I said, "You mean like a silver bullet?" intending to sound clever and witty and upbeat on the comeback like he always did. But since she hadn't watched that late-night, round-the-clock weekend-long marathon of those ancient *Lone Ranger* reruns with Jimmy and me on the flat-screen TV he'd carted in, I don't think she got what I meant. She compressed her lips, her shoulders tightening, and stared off as I described how the door to the outbuilding had been left wide open and that the space was empty now.

"For Pete's sake," she said, but did not press for any additional details. She nodded, took her polar fleece from the coat tree, and said, "Show me," the field behind the outbuilding windswept and the temperature already well below freezing.

She entered first, allowed for her open eye to adjust, and said, "Other than for this?" And she picked up the padlock, which I hadn't noticed, left right there on the 4x8 makeshift plywood table. Minus the combination code, I figured, we had about as much chance of cracking it as we did figuring out Jimmy's whereabouts or intentions, and the odds of his return seemed remote to me.

My mom was wearing her pirate patch, and the day was fast fading away. I could see her breath in the air. Behind us the wind kept sucking the door open and banging it closed. Like maybe the sheriff's department deputies, tipped off and with a warrant in hand, were kicking it down.

I wish they had. And that they'd described in their report how a sudden glint of wintery light on its low downward slide through the window momentarily turned my mom's face bronze, how there was no sign of any spoils, the floor swept and a few extra sawhorses stacked against the far wall, and this, in case it seemed important: the sound of snow pinging against the metal roof, and the two of us just staring up and listening.

LAND OF THE
LOST AND FOUND

I'D ESTIMATE a couple-three years *after* the real-estate venture went
belly up was when we moved in. A tire iron instead of a front door
key and the padlock so flimsy it popped on the first try, as if anxious
to share in the trouble Sheila guaranteed was ours for the taking. I'd
pledged better. Respectable full time employment, health benefits, a
401(k). That life. Commonsense and better managed. Given that we'd
been camping out in the van, and my wife of six years curling farther
and farther away from me each night under the queen-size comforter,
knees tight to her chest, our love life on hold.

And Sheila not saying, "Good night." Not saying, "Sweet dreams,"
or "Tomorrow's another day," but rather, "Any freaking port in a
storm, right, Fletch?" And her tone making clear that what we needed
was a practical backup plan for a change, a shingled roof over our
heads and an actual doorway to step through together if there was any
chance whatsoever of returning again to our happier selves.

Annulment I'd heard of, but a reverse *marriage*? I swear to God
that's how she phrased it after our eviction for back rent unpaid. And
the pot plants—a thriving quarter-acre plot of them—suddenly pul-
verized worthless in the recent, deep-drench downpours. Rain and
wind and hail straight out of the Bible, sideways chuting sheets of it
unlike anything we'd ever endured out here on the far northern tip of

nowhere. Had there been a creek or stream nearby, the house trailer would have lifted from its moorings like an ark and floated away.

Amateur growers. First-timers in the medical marijuana trade, but Sheila with a green thumb and with our future pulsing dimmer with each passing day, I argued, "What's to lose? I mean, okay, so we're unlicensed, I get that part." I deemed it a minor technicality and a far cry from peddling meth or pilfered pharmaceuticals along the downtrodden, single-stoplight towns that bordered us.

"Spare me," she said. "Never fails, does it? The crackpot theories, the bullshit rationale," though next thing I knew we'd started the plants from seeds in a makeshift atrium. They could have been anything—zinnias or sunflowers or even zucchini—and one late May morning on our hands and knees we patted the soil in the furrows around each spindly stem. One after the other, hour after hour and taking a break at the end of each row we'd ballpark our potential gross, not in joints or Ziploc ounces but in monster kilo multiples.

We referred to it as our Field of Dreams and agreed when the plants reached three feet and budding up we'd coast into our new lifestyle absent any stress or anxiety, and, first and foremost, we'd shit-can our grind-it-out, spirit-killing day jobs. Sheila from Bojack's Bar and Grill, with its borderline starvation wages if you included the tips and subtracted the foot miles. And me, not a trained orderly but a janitor, scrubbing and then swabbing a mop back and forth across the shiny black-and-white-checkerboard hallways of Mission Ridge, a rest home that specialized in advanced Alzheimer's care for widows and widowers. And where pet-friendly meant being awakened most nights by the distant, forlorn choruses of coyotes. On any given shift, a sure bet that I'd be mistaken half a dozen times, minimum, for someone's son or grandson or even their own fathers at thirty-one, stopping by for a visit.

We'd discussed having children—Sheila and me—and we followed the conversation forward: the names and nicknames we'd give them. Smart, ambitious kids who'd answer the call to scrap vocational for college prep and full-ride academic scholarships. Living proof that against the odds we'd raised them right. Our own flesh and blood living professional lives in exotic locales like Cincinnati or Chicago. Or maybe even Corpus Christi, Texas, where rumor had it you could make a killing as an offshore driller on one of those monster sea derricks in the Gulf of Mexico. I'd even brainstormed heading down there some winter, scoping it out. Pocketing a seasonal payload, and, for once in my life, being able to say to Sheila, "Here, buy yourself something nice," like a pair of pricey sunglasses or a genuine, soft leather handbag, and believing each impulse purchase would constitute a small down payment on a loving and durable and time-tested married life. Maybe do a little surf fishing. But when I pitched the idea all she said was, "Go Aggies," and it's already been a long slog since she last shimmied out of her cutoffs or blue jeans in front of me, Mr. Big-Plans Family Man.

Instead, rewind to the two of us flat busted and sharing a Pall Mall. Passing it back and forth, rationing what was left in the pack and staring out the window all the way to the tail end of that interminable deluge. When finally after a straight week it stopped, I joked, "Time to send out the birds, near about," and up flew her two middle fingers.

"What'd you call it, working smart? Making it happen? That *is* what you said, is it not? That what doesn't kill us will only make us stronger? Well, let the record show," she said. By which she meant par for the course, and that my every ambition had its roots in delusion and self-destruction and that we couldn't, if we tried, have been more wrong for each other.

"We'll get it right," I said. "We'll be fine, no worries there." But she's a believer in omens and signs, and themes repeated, and so even after the weather flipped back to blue skies and sunshine, I calculated that wasn't the moment for another get-rich-quick scheme, but rather for some major fixing up on the domestic front.

We used to talk often, a meeting of the minds to try and reset our sights realistically. But somewhere not all that far back we'd turned distant and nonverbal in ways that had given legs to the unthinkable.

And so I said, "Whoa, back up a minute. You mean a reverse *mortgage*, not a reverse *marriage*, right?" knowing full well that we might still be half a century removed from that. If the future went according to plan, and I wanted more than anything for the two of us to arrive there together, with our hearts intact.

"Not hardly," she said. "No, not anymore." Thing was, and as I reminded her, *had* that cash crop been harvested, had we sealed the deal, she'd be flashing a full carat and a half on her ring finger like one of those CNN anchorwomen. We're talking drop-dead gorgeous, and front-facing in something low-cut, I swear, she'd send those network ratings skyward, the viewers hypnotized, tuning in evening after evening, no matter how retched the weather or the world news, just to see that darker red outlining those full and slightly, perfectly parted lips.

Not that she craved the spotlight. And for sure not while we were up to no good, her arms crossed, head down, and leaning against the van as I pumped some midgrade, long-billed ball caps pulled low and the Dixie Chicks no more than a pulse from some faraway country-western station.

She pointed at the warning sign—DRIVE-OFFS DON'T DRIVE IN MICHIGAN—as if to remind me of what we were doing, the price we were likely to pay. "Uh-huh," I said. "But hey, look on the bright side. At least the plates are valid. There's that," as if stashed somewhere in our past was an extra set for petty capers in times as lonely and as desperate as these.

That's when she came at me, right there under the surveillance cameras, all fists and elbows and knees. And wearing short-shorts and electric-blue imitation snakeskin cowgirl boots, and a sleeveless T-shirt she'd brocaded, front and back, with hundreds of tiny blistered glass beads. I pictured the cashier smacking her gum, lifting the phone from its cradle, the sheriff's department deputies already on their way. Which is what I said, pleading with her, as in fifty-thousand-volt Tasers, and handcuffs and separate holding cells. Strip searches, arraignments, and fines. A public defender who couldn't give a flying fuck about our kind, and finally calming her down we scrounged enough pocket change for half a tank, some Slim Jims, and a six-pack of ice-cold Old Milwaukee for the road.

"I'll be right back," I said. "Okay?" And I steered her to the passenger side and kissed her through the open window, the two of us still wild-eyed and panting. "Sit tight. I've got this," and while I paid I watched the mini-mart monitor, our high-mileage nondescript Chevy van in which we'd first dated, its easy idle and rusty bumper hitch, as if to remind myself that we were *not* Mickey and Mallory, natural born killers on a rampage of love. We were Sheila Beal and Fletcher Ray and not a single arrest or outstanding warrant between us. At worst a couple of speeding tickets, a parking violation or two. Plus more than a few mostly regrettable, ugly thoughts I'd entertained from time to time on the off chance of someday getting even with Billy Skeets, my ex stepfather, who married my mom when I was five.

Unlike him I am neither hostile nor foul-tempered, and I have never been prone to random, unprovoked anger or violence. Though having been witness to it, blow by drunken blow to my mom and sometimes to me if I tried to protect her, I understand firsthand how rage erupts not *necessarily* out of the blue, but rather from some slow, spooky-calm, premeditated need and intent. Followed by the after threats, the taunts and accusations. The pure and furious undisguised contempt.

And the way he'd sometimes enter my bedroom in the pitch dark and flick the blue sulfur heads of stick matches with his thumbnail, each hissing flame reflected in those flat, colorless, mutantlike eyes that blinked maybe once every five minutes. Like he was asleep and awake at the same time, the arteries at his temples pulsing. He'd say nothing, as if it fell to me and me alone to interpret the menace of him looming bedside and staring down at me while he nursed another rum on the rocks.

Although indicted he was never convicted for setting the worst fire in the town's history. No eyewitnesses. No one with firsthand infor mation willing to place him at the crime scene and the five-gallon gas can in the garage still three-quarters full.

A hung jury, though I'd wager to this day that he's the one who torched the insurance agency, where those two priceless, vintage 1948 Vincent Black Shadow motorcycles he coveted and cursed were showcased. He'd kidnap me—that's what he called it—and we'd stop there two, three times a week, and he'd say, "Helluva tease, ain't it?" He'd say, "Jeezus," and we'd get out of the truck, rain or shine, and eyeball them from the sidewalk, the blinding polished chrome handlebars, oversize carburetors, tailpipes, and chain guards. Spokes that appeared to hum and spin under the bright spotlights. Spellbound is what he was. Wouldn't move a muscle or even breathe, his forehead deep-creased like he was thinking dangerous, impossible-to-pull-off thoughts. After maybe a full couple of minutes he'd say, "That'd fit the bill real good now, wouldn't it? You and me hell-bound on some endless highway the fuck away from here." And he'd talk about how he'd beat the damn brakes off anyone told us otherwise. "Just let 'em try," he'd say, his lips mere inches from the plate glass, which was thick enough, as he said, to withstand the full-force, high-impact swing of a forty-ounce Louisville Slugger. And possibly double-barreled buckshot fired point-blank, his Remington twelve-gauge loaded and racked across the pickup's rear window in all seasons.

MY MOM'S MAIDEN NAME is Wemigwans. She's half Ottawa, which makes me a quarter, what Billy Skeets called a breed apart. What I called him, though never to his face, was a waste of skin in any tribe or nationality.

My real father, and namesake, was killed in a car wreck two months before I was born. Except for a D- in chemistry, my mom says I inherited his smarts and good looks, her raven hair and high cheekbones, the warm, coppery blood we sometimes tasted. Not to mention the shared bruises and black eyes along the way, though I never, like her, had a detached retina. Billy Skeets, he who drank and leered and berated us as freaks and freeloaders. "Like it or not," he said. "That's the two of you sure and simple. Takers." And I'd think the exact same thing he was thinking. As in, and good goddamn riddance to you, too.

Why we stayed as long as we did I haven't a clue, except I wanted nothing to do with foster care, nor wherever it was she left for, an unspecified location way out of range of Thompsonville. For her own protection, she said, although by then I'd all but dared him to lift a hand or balled fist or obstruct anyone's path to the refrigerator or bathroom or TV. I'd turned seventeen, a broad-shouldered high school senior on the wrestling team and already on *my* way elsewhere.

I watched her leave with no more than an overnight case, while Billy Skeets hefted fifty-pound bags of shelled corn onto the loading platform of the feed and grain exchange where he moonlighted a couple fill in days each week. I almost said, "Mom, don't go. Please, no. We'll file abuse charges and get a restraining order against him." But as if she were reading my mind, she pressed her index finger to her lips, shook her head, her eyes watery, and exited without a single backward glance at me.

Just last year Billy Skeets busted out of Alger Correctional, a few hours north across the Straits, and was apprehended later that same day. Unarmed but still dangerous and resisting arrest and now—count them—a *three*-time loser. I'd read about it in the local newspaper, saw the photo of him in handcuffs, that same embittered smirk. If I'd had a magnifying glass, I could have read the numbers on his prison jumpsuit. Another eight years added to his sentence and, as you can imagine, for crimes way worse than attempted theft at the local gas pump. And, for the sake of rescuing my marriage, this B&E. If my mom ever *were* to somehow contact me, I'd tell her that it's been safe for a while now for her to come out of hiding. And that wherever she hailed from these days, I'd very much like to drive there, no matter how far. Just to catch up, good or bad, on what all the years have done to our lives.

I'D FIRST COME across the place while hunting grouse and woodcock last fall, a three-set cluster of streamside A-frames in different stages of unfinished. From cracked slab and exposed rebar to half-framed in to almost complete. Simple, single-room layouts, and the only dividing wall the one for the bathroom. I cased each structure. Imagined the deal as somebody's build-and-flip—another mad genius on a money grab and the housing market *still* trenching lower in these parts. Forgottens and giveaways. Teardowns if the recovery ever were to spill out this way, though long gone were the odds of that happening anytime soon.

There'd been wind gusts out of the north, a cold front moving in and the leaves mostly down and no birds bursting skyward from the underbrush, the hunting season one day from over. When I pressed my forehead to the slider I could feel the winter bite of the breeze vibrate across the wavy glass. I couldn't see a whole lot inside, but I was all about the wraparound deck, and so I sat for a while in the lazy, late-afternoon sunshine, blaze-orange vest and hat, and a shotgun in the crook of my arm. I might even have mentioned it to Sheila, a potential artist's studio, plus a deep downstream pool where I'd spotted half a dozen decent-size brook trout.

It wouldn't have taken much—a quick scrubdown, some inexpensive window blinds. Sawhorses, a couple of 4x8 sheets of plywood, then build the inventory and export Sheila's jewelry to all those upscale tourist boutiques along the Lake Michigan coastline. Towns with sidewalks and gas lamps, summer mansions, the lawns stretching all the way to the water. Sheila had never taken her jewelry making all that seriously. More like a hobby that generated a few extra bucks from time to time. Barrettes, bracelets, bangles, and pendants, and earrings decorated with a single semiprecious gemstone or two.

After the road beers and my apology for whatever it was worth, Sheila nodded and left unmentioned the mess-ups she'd no doubt been tallying back to the day we met. Even as we bumped up the quarter mile of rutted, overgrown two-track and across a narrow bridge, she remained silent. But as soon as I killed the headlights she said, "Good God Almighty." She said, "How'd we ever get reduced to this? How in the world did we end up *here?*"

She sounded on the verge of tears, cranked up her window, and I thought, *From all four compass points, that's how,* and I pointed to the stars through the high-up sprays and tree branches. And to the moon, full risen and bone white and everywhere around us the blinking asses of a million fireflies in perfect mirror mode of the northern lights.

"We're almost there," I said. "Another few minutes max." And like clockwork the A-frame suddenly in stark and naked silhouette right in front of us. "If it spooks you we're out of here," I said. "Simple as that, you just say the word." And she nodded again as I exited the van, not brandishing the tire iron though in no way concealing what I had in mind. I could hear the slow lap and burble of the stream, the throaty, low burping of bullfrogs, the distant hooting of an owl.

Like I said, an easy entry, the door as screechy on its hinges as fighting feral cats. Why I closed it behind me I'm not sure. Maybe to keep out any dive-bombing bats or ghosts, and the moon-glow through the hexagonal skylight silvering the steep interior roof pitch of the walls almost blue, the smell dank and loamy and shut in like a cave. Nothing you needed to hold your breath against, or that couldn't be aired out with a window fan, a simple tap-in to the electrical line and bingo, a breathable free space in which to lay low for a while.

I groped for the light switch anyway, flipped it as if a lamp or overhead might magically ignite, and then I waited for my eyes to adjust, a mere matter of minutes before the room started to widen around me. A corner fireplace and a sleeping loft on stilts. Freestanding like a forest fire lookout, and a ladder to climb dead tired into bed. A kitchen island minus the drawers and countertop, and no cupboards or appliances or any furniture, as if the place had been ransacked, stripped bare, contents sold off or repossessed. Had Sheila entered with me, had I carried her across the threshold second-honeymoon style, she'd have mad scrambled the luck out of my arms and made straight for the van. Blown a good-bye kiss to this deadbeat life of ours and driven away and most likely forever, and truth be told I wouldn't have blamed her one bit.

And this: a swing suspended from the cross-braces. Not a slow mom-and-pop glider-type, but rather a single seat. Like that one on the park playground where, sleepless some humid summer nights after we'd first tied the knot, we used to walk, hand in hand, in our T-shirts and pajama shorts, and where Sheila would say, "Top or bottom?" Our standing joke, and then she'd place her palms on my shoulders and rotate her hips back and forth until she'd straddled me, the two of us cinched in tight. I'm six-foot-three, and she'd say, "Harder," and we'd pump and pump until the balls of our feet at the apex of each ascending arc seemed always to pause for a tick or two, our bodies weightless. And the way we'd kiss, our tongues alternately pressed to the roof of each other's mouth like gravity itself. That was the miracle life I wanted back, the entire universe tumbling in reverse circles around us.

"Home free," I said when I got back to the van. "The place, it's totally deserted." And no flashlight or lantern, naturally, but under a hunter's moon I figured we'd get settled in okay, haul the foam mat inside, the comforter and pillows, and the night, as I saw it, maybe not entirely lost or forsaken after all. Her feet stayed pressed to the dashboard, and her head cocked against the seat rest, her entire body gone rigid.

"Cook in or go out?" she wisecracked, and without making eye contact she drained the last of her three Old Milwaukees and tossed the empty can over her shoulder into the cluttered rear.

"Really, it's not half-bad," I said. "Especially on our budget. No blindfold necessary." But she didn't for one second soften or stop shaking her head.

Instead she said, "The toilets still plunge the same way, do they?" A reference to a duplex we'd once rented, the plumbing shot, the busted flush valve, drains plugged, and I said, "Listen, I admit it. It's a far cry from perfect, but we can work the pieces. I'm positive we can puzzle this together." As if to prove me a liar, she opened the van door, stepped out, dropped her shorts, squatted, and peed in the knee-high weeds and ostrich ferns.

"So this is what we've become. Squatters," she said. "And what happens when whoever owns this shithole shows up?"

"Adverse possession," I said. "And possession being nine-tenths of the law. It's a basic fact. You make claim to it, it's yours for the taking." A legal term I'd heard Billy Skeets misuse one time when we'd trespassed in some guy's barn and heisted half a dozen antique milking tins, which he then turned into ready cash—what he called wampum—for a couple fifths of cheap rum but claimed a bigger pay-off was headed our way. "Soon as you got the soul for it," he said. "Soon as you're ready." I hated having said what I did, as if I'd taken his lying side against the person I loved and trusted and needed most in this uncertain life.

"One night," Sheila said. "And only because I'm exhausted and half-drunk. And depressed and hungry for an actual meal, and I don't mean junk food or leftovers only a goat could choke down. I'm talking about meals fixed in our own damn kitchen. A dining room table and matching silverware. A phone with a dial tone. The rest, whatever you're selling, I'm not buying it and I don't care. I'm done. First thing tomorrow morning I'll hand-deliver my updated resume. Who knows, maybe third time's the charm."

I knew she meant the Recovery Room, a roadhouse where she'd waitressed twice before but ditched out because of the double shifts and the catcalls and the jukebox so loud you couldn't convey a single word of conversation, your throat hoarse and gritty from trying. A menu of beer batter and deep fry. The life we'd run from, and which, in all likelihood, she'd now—and blame this one on me, guilty as charged—beg back.

WHAT WOKE ME was the sound of something squeaking, and when I half-opened my eyelids Sheila's ass orbited by as if a part of the sun had broken free, and the skylight, directly above me, ablaze like a tunnel of molten fire. I had zero recollection of where I was, trapped somewhere, I reasoned, on the edge of those old nightmare sweats and screams, except that no one *was* screaming, my T-shirt dry, no sheets knotted around me. I sat up slowly, and dizzy-eyed I followed her descent and backward rise, and dangled my legs off the side of the bed, and Sheila's naked body in a slow-motion glide, right toward me, nostrils flared and her hair braided and trailing like a thick and shiny golden tail. She shouted, "Stay out of my way," and when she reached for something stowed behind the highest crossbeam, that sudden, wicked vertigo I used to suffer as a kid kicked in. Like a seizure. Trembles and black flashes like you get holding your breath underwater too long, lungs constricting, and then your eyes closing on a gazillion tiny exploding multicolored halos and orbs.

When I came to, Sheila was sitting Indian-style right beside me, and the world was sparkling like sequins. I blindered my hands around my eyes and said, "Sheila, where the Christ are we?"

"They're real," she said. "Diamonds and cultured pearls and emeralds and stones I can't identify. And feast your eyes on this. A vintage rose-gold wristwatch engraved with someone's initials. Someone B.A.M. I wound it, listen," she said and pressed the crystal to my ear. I'd never heard such faraway and slowed-down ticking of the seconds.

I'd only ever seen Sheila decked out in cheap, cut-rate make-believes, the costume kind she designed to *kill* time while rushing ahead in her mind into what she called a normal, halfway decent home life. "Is that too much to ask?" she'd say. And it shouldn't have been, not then and not ever. It's what I believed in, too, whether my life reflected that or not: Tiki lamps and a gas grill, and low-slung lawn chairs, our feet propped on a Kmart cooler of cold ones. The lazy, undulating wave of a sprinkler breaking across our *own* backyard at dusk, a couple tired kids to tuck into bed.

Our birthdays, they're only five calendar days apart, although Sheila's two years older. She's thirty-three and keeps careful count on what she calls her body clock and the seasons in their perpetual rolling away. "Do the math," she'd say, as if we'd already bargained away too much, every holiday from Valentine's to next Christmas merely adding to the diminished expectations that shaped our lives. There were mornings she would eat her cereal with her eyes closed, as if there had to be a better reason to get out of bed and face the day.

And here it was late August again, and she said, "Fletch, pay close attention to what I'm saying, okay?"

I squinted even harder, her body a tangle of jeweled snakes. She'd painted her fingernails and reapplied her lipstick, the chartreuse and crimson refracting wildly from all the rings, the bracelets up to her elbows. Necklaces and earrings that shimmered and strobed if she so much as nodded, let alone leaned in so close that our eyelashes touched.

"There's enough money in this to last us half a lifetime," she whispered, as if the thieves or the law were right outside, the slider open, and Sheila dressed like a chandelier, a dark-grained, oversize mahogany jewelry box balanced on her lap.

She opened the velvet-lined top, then each drawer, and started to unclasp one priceless piece at a time. "Possibly it's even ours by rights if what you said is true. Adverse possession," she said, and although I nodded all I could think was to wipe her fingerprints off everything she'd touched, evidence that someone, somewhere, could end up using against us.

THE FIRST SNOWFALL arrived in mid-October and the carved pumpkins on the front stoop of our new digs smiled their flickering orange glow. We liked the location well enough on the town's outskirts, though not so much the for-sale-by-owner terms. Meaning the full asking price in a dying market, and a substantial enough down payment to negate my seasonal employment installing for Invisible Fence.

"We're good for it," I said, and he just nodded, and then cocked and handed over a ballpoint pen. And like signing a confession, Sheila and I provided our John Hancocks above a binding foreclosure clause should we fail, for any reason, to cough up on the first day of each month every hard-earned red cent we owed him.

In return, a standard-issue starter-upper three-bedroom ranch, a bath and a half, and a white birch clump in our backyard. A breezeway and a carport and a roadside mailbox with our last names stenciled in red across both sides. We stocked the refrigerator first thing. Including a roll of quarters for the freezer, which, some late evenings after applying for jobs other than waitressing, Sheila—sometimes heads, sometimes tails—would press to her eyelids. I'd keep the sound on the TV down, the two of us on the couch, her head on my lap. "Back from the brink" is how Sheila phrased it.

Her name, the victim of the robbery? Beverly Anne Moses, a seventy-seven-year-old widow, living alone. No children and her husband deceased nearly a decade. "The facts, ma'am, just the facts," as Sergeant Joe Friday used to say on those *Dragnet* reruns I sometimes watched with my mom and Billy Skeets during infrequent stretches when the three of us pretended to get along.

A forced entry, the two ski-masked ex-cons from downstate with rap sheets a mile long, reform school in their early teens, Jackson maximum security in their midtwenties. Sheila's got skills enough that we viewed their mug shots on the local library computer, read newspaper accounts of the crime and the arrests one week later, the stolen credit cards in the glove box of their Dodge Ram. A handgun. The roll of duct tape they used to restrain Mrs. Moses in a chair in a corner, a gag in her mouth, and the jewelry still missing. They were serving eighteen to twenty, without the possibility of parole.

We figured that provided us enough time to negotiate the swap and get the full, originally offered-up cash reward. And case closed, no names, and no questions asked. No easy chatter, I promised myself. The exchange would be detached, matter-of-fact, businesslike. And I wouldn't take one step deeper into the house than absolutely necessary. Just get there and get gone, although she did invite me in first thing when I tapped the heavy brass knocker, Sheila waiting in the getaway van two blocks away.

I'd formulated no picture of her, just a blank, black-and-white space in my mind, closed off to imagination. I wished there'd been a way not to see her at all, but she'd insisted on face-to-face. Just the two of us and I'd agreed.

I wore my baseball cap and sweatshirt, carried the jewelry box like a miniature wooden suitcase under one arm. I stood back when the front door opened, the wind brisk and hissing off Lake Michigan.

"So, it's you," she said, as if she'd picked me out of a lineup. "And so punctual. Welcome," she said, "to the land of the lost and found."

I entered but only as far as the rug in the foyer, though from there I could see into the living room, a shiny black baby grand piano, and a wine bottle holding a single red rose.

"I think this belongs to you," I said, and I handed over the jewels and the watch. I imagined it ticking inside like a tiny silver and gold heart.

"Please, put it down right there," she said, "on the end table. Next to the reward money."

I nodded and did what she said. "And this, too. I'm sorry." And I relinquished the ring I'd earlier slipped into my pants pocket. Collateral in case things fouled in some unanticipated way. "That's all. The rest," I said. "Everything's there."

"Ah," she said. "Yes. And I trust not for someone with fingers like these?" Palms down she held out both shaky hands toward me, the gnarled and swollen knuckles, and the top joints of each finger hinged and canted at impossible angles. "My husband would be forever grateful. Whoever you are, he'd insist. So, for him—and for me, too—you keep it. As you can see, I've got plenty of others I can't wear anymore, either."

The entire transaction took less than ten minutes, and then I had, in my possession, twenty-five grand. We'd driven two hours to get there, and true or not we'd convinced ourselves that we'd hurt no one, broken no laws. And yet the entire way up to Harbor Springs I felt panicky, predatory, guilty and sad and lonely and exposed, thinking, *What have we gotten ourselves into?* What my mom might have referred to as dread. I even balked when Mrs. Moses gestured toward the thick envelope of bills. Written across the front in a kind of tangled cursive, the word *Rescuer*.

"What was she like?" Sheila asked when I got back. "Eccentric, am I right? She'd have to be," as if the transfer had occurred as Mrs. Moses sipped bubbly while she soaked in a claw-foot bathtub.

"She was beautiful." That's what I said to Sheila. "She wished us well." I said that, too, and when Sheila said back, "You counted the money?" I turned on the dome light, lifted her hand, and slid the ring onto her finger. "It's all there," I said, though I'd yet to even look inside. "And this, it's a bonus, a gift. Nothing I pilfered. So you know."

I started the engine and swung a U-turn back the way we'd come. Past Turtle Creek Casino, where, out of habit, I'd normally hit the brakes, the blinker. Turn in, skim from the top what I figured we could afford to lose and still be okay. Or win. No question that I could have persuaded Sheila. A free drink or two, and then we'd grab a seat at the blackjack or poker table.

Instead, we drove right by, the morning already coming on. For a while neither of us said another thing. I lit a cigarette, cracked the window. I knew what she was thinking, that possibly our luck really was, against the odds, changing in some better way. The traffic was light and with the stars suddenly in free fall she held the diamond up tight to the windshield. Like a compass, I thought. Like a tiny blinking satellite in the force field of what, and who, we believed was us.

THE GOOD FATHER

MY DAD'S NAME is Philly Penwaydon and, meaning to be funny, he's started addressing me, his estranged and only son, as Sam Lee P., like I'm part Korean or something. I'm not. I'm black Irish on my mom's side, clear blue eyes and hair the color of onyx. On my dad's, American mutt, and, from what I've been able to piece together, mostly pinscher and Rottweiler, minus the choke chain and rabies shots.

My mom and I live in Grand Rapids, where she teaches sign language at the school for the deaf. Which *she* is not, nor am I, though whenever she wants me to listen extra close to what she's saying, she'll talk in that patient, silent slow dance of her fingers and hands. I understand some of what she says, but even those parts that I miss—I know they're no less forgiving about my dad.

He's been out of prison for a full year following his parole, long enough without incident to warrant this visit, my first, even against my mom's repeated objections and appeals. "Okay, enough. I'm worn out, Sam Lee," she eventually said and, legal adult or not, deferred the final decision to me. It took all of about two seconds because no matter how you argue it, you can't train or command a kid like me away from his own flesh and blood.

I'm not exactly in partnership with him, not yet, though this morning he said, "Good job," as I tramped down the grass and weeds on the side of the highway, a two-lane with no center stripe and tons of rubber. That's so people driving by can read the telephone number on the Affordable Stump Grinding signs we staked every quarter mile all the way south to Mesick and back. Some within a few yards of those stark-white death crosses. There are way more than seems normal, like maybe it's where the bored-crazy teenagers drag race or play chicken. The crosses are kind of eerie, all decorated with garlands and plastic wreaths and rosaries. And one with bright-yellow graduation tassels that fluttered in the breeze.

The way my dad first described it over the telephone, I imagined the stump grinder as some Godzilla-like monstrosity he'd junked together. Wheels and gears and saw-blade jawbones that could pulverize, in a matter of minutes, the ancient root balls of oaks, and ironwood, and black walnut. Or even the petrified deadfall in the shallow coves of Lake Tonawanda, where we used to walleye fish before my mom and me moved away when I was ten, that same year my dad began serving his sentence at Camp Pugsley. We never visited him, not once during all that time, and to my surprise and disappointment he has not violated the restraining order against him by hightailing it back to us. My mom swears that if he ever tries, she'll press charges to the full extent of the law. And, as she admitted to me last night, it's the price that men who've grimed up their lives like this pay in grief and shame for their freedom.

He's a torch welder by trade but out of work since last May when the junkyard went belly-up. It's where all the ghost cars used to get towed, he explained, and said that one time he salvaged from the wreckage a wedding band embedded in steel, a tiny round vein of gold right there in the mangled manifold. "And Jesus H. All-Merciful Christ," he said. "No way on this earth could I hazard the make or model. Some damn import or other, a Peugeot or Mercedes—I don't know." Not that he could stay alive on strikes such as these and, to emphasize that point, he tap-tapped his temple with the tip of his index finger, as if to make clear that, *Here's how you survive, Sam Lee P. Up here's your future pure and simple.*

According to my mom he's smart all right, and that's what's got her worried. The way his mind always works a good idea bad, and I figure what we're up to might constitute a prime example. Him drinking Old Milwaukee, I mean, and waiting around for the phone to ring even though a single drop of alcohol violates his parole, as my mom never ceases to remind me. But go ahead, try telling him that it's illegal to toast our time together after so long apart, and see how that results in anything worthwhile.

A *working* vacation's what he calls it, and management means fringe benefits, "And here's to us," he says, "the owners and inventors," and he takes another swig, the water tower the only blue patch in the bruised sky, and some not-so-far-off lightning and rumble. We're outside, facing each other from opposite ends of the johnboat, the Coleman cooler between us. Like we've just pushed away from shore in a slow drift out toward the drop-off, our lines trailing, the blood-fat black leeches squirming on our hooks, and a net and tape measure on the seat beside me.

That's what I've wished for in his absence and I still do—to be out on the water like we used to. "Soon enough," he says, as if now that *I'm* here all we need to do is put our heads together and anything's possible.

The boat is up on cinderblocks in this partially fenced-in backyard, and the property backed up almost all the way to the old tri-county landfill, seventy-some odd acres worth my dad says. The property is lush and contoured and shiny green as a treeless rain forest against the unforgiving doldrums.

The construction trailer he's renting is only temporary, summer digs as spare as a platform tent. Like camping out, he says, except for the flush toilet and cold-water tap. A hot plate for a kitchen and everything beer-basted and pan-fried, and the only door propped open with a brick, so we're not entirely roughing it.

No shrubs or flower boxes, no birdhouses either, like back home, and there's one of those corkscrew metal stakes in the ground, and a chain attached as if he's got in mind to buy me a goat or 4-H heifer for all those consecutive birthdays that he's missed. But I'm well beyond all that. After all, I'm in tenth grade, beginning this September, six inches taller now, and my dad finally off the leash with the law. Changes such as these—they don't occur overnight, and, if logic holds, who in God's name *would* care enough anymore to check up on the two of us so shut off from all worlds other than our own? My mom, I suppose, but against those odds I'd wager our entire bankroll once word spreads and the business catches hold.

He says, "You want to guess on our first score's purchase?" but before I can answer he adds, "A set of oars, and some caulk to seal the bottom leaks. A couple new rods and backlash-free Bait-Master reels wouldn't hurt the cause, either, would they? And then just live the good life as good as it gets and anchor the past back there behind us, where it belongs."

I hope we can, but he's already been fishing around for information about what my mom's been up to. She's still pretty as ever—tall, slim waist, thirty-seven—and, as of a couple Decembers ago, officially single again.

Unlike my dad, whose hand I shook but who I barely recognized when I first stepped off the Greyhound, she hasn't aged at all. Really, cast back four years, before the trial and the guilty as charged, and there she is, bare-shouldered and dangling her feet over the square-nosed stern of a boat not unlike this one in better days. Eyes closed, her legs long and thin—relive *that* afternoon, everyone wins out. I've got a snapshot to prove it's true. Not on me, of course, and how cruel anyway would it be to hold it up, like an image of her both here and not here in the brutal-sad and maximum extreme.

It's mid-August and sweltering hot, and he's wearing those hand wraps he uses to pummel the heavy oxblood bag suspended from the single-bay garage rafter, where he stores his acetylene tank and his mask and tools. Anger management's what I figure, but all I know for sure is that whenever he digs a single left hook, that sweaty leather wheezes and it's easy to imagine the sudden cave-in of a man's ribs. And the practical matter thereafter and therefore forever, as my mom insists, of having a felon in our family. "An ex-con, Sam Lee, and no matter what he says or promises, that trail never goes cold entirely."

The way she carries on you'd think that he'd killed a man with his bare fists, but he didn't. Nor, as she readily admits, has he ever raised one toward her or me, and so where's the threat is the question that I want considered. Nowhere, as far as I can tell, and some judge ever gives me the third degree, I'll testify under oath that one-on-one my dad and me, we make a pretty formidable team.

His crime? Breaking and entering. And the premeditated destruction of property, which he'd never condone unprovoked, but you deny someone like him with dreams and aspirations a small business loan, he might not just tuck his tail between his haunches and cower away. It made the national news. The bank president back from Florida, and his vintage, cherry-red 1956 T-Bird transformed into a BBQ mobile. The trunk and passenger-side door torched shut and, mounted on the hood, a backyard barrel grill, the cover raised and, inside, the best revenge detail of all: a swollen-up, shiny, copper-plated hotdog with one end fluted like the top of someone's penis. And a spray-painted sign along the front and rear panels that said, all in capital letters, BIG WEENIES ARE BETTER. My buddy, Boyd Tuggle, still cracks up just thinking about it, but truth told, you witness your dad handcuffed and forcibly removed from the house, and your sense of humor laughs itself out awful fast.

His squint lines—they're road maps to nowhere I ever want to end up is what he tells me. It's as close as he's come to describing his incarceration, the grooves deepening in his forehead whenever he lights up a Pall Mall. And his thumb's much jerkier on the butane striker than I remember, like he might blow a fuse any second, and the smoke held so long in his lungs that almost nothing comes out on the exhales.

He's inquired about school. All A's, all subjects, history my favorite. And I guess, if you leap ahead another year, a driver's permit is in the works, but uh-uh, no girlfriend to slide right up tight to me on the slippery vinyl seat of my mom's Ford Falcon. "It'll happen," he says. "Trust me." Which I do, though the only girl who's ever even kissed me is Novella Delzel. On the neck, while we slow-danced in the basement of the Second Congregational Church, a private personal detail you'd never confess to any adult, except possibly at gunpoint.

"How 'bout your mom, *she* seeing someone?" he asks now. Casual, off-the-cuff sounding, but I don't take the bait straight away, and I don't lie, either. Instead, I describe how she sometimes silently sings herself to sleep on the couch, her lips and fingertips twitching some made-up tune she'll later teach to those school kids.

He nods, like, Okay, fair enough, and yeah, there have been men, but not a long list, and only one weekend live-in, and in the end that turned out to be short-term anyhow. A guy I liked—a Vietnam vet with a prosthetic arm, but mention him and that hateful war that recently ended, and my dad will go gale-force. That's what my mom warned, but other than railing on the heavy bag, I haven't witnessed any such evidence, and his sense of humor up to this point refutes *that* charge. "Just remember," she said, "stay vague when it comes to me, Sam Lee. Do not push that button." And then in sign, her fist hitting the breakfast table like a soundless gavel, "Please promise me that. For everyone's sake."

Luckily, the sky keeps darkening, and I point toward the storm-blow no longer a county or two distant, the thunderclaps smack dab above us. "Whoa, listen to that," I say, the treetops in full bend and weave, and I make a joke about how this just might turn out to be the windfall we're after. Even the boat rocks a little, and when my dad breaks loose with laughter in the sudden downpour, it's not so unlike old times. Minus my mom, that is, and the gray in his hair, and no lifejackets, and him standing up, which he always instructed me never to do, not even if the rod throbbed and bent double.

I hold onto both sides for balance as he steps down, the rain smacking the ground muddy all around us, like the oval-mouthed frenzy of thousands and thousands of feeding fish.

THERE'S A FIFTY-GALLON DRUM that's attached to the backside of the roof, plus a pipe and showerhead. No pressure to speak of, but the rainwater's warm, and so I'm still in the makeshift stall, staring up at the full moon as bright as I've ever seen it, and shooting stars galore. My dad—he's the one who taught me their names, washed kind of murky lately, but Orion's easy to identify on a night like this. And I'm pretty certain that's the Quail's Head, and there's the Barking Dog, which you can't ever hear or summon, but the landfill's been growling like my dad said it does late in the summer, following heavy weather like yesterday and today. Rain turned hail, and high humidity, and temperatures right out of Hades. He claims if you press your ear to the ground after midnight, you'll hear the heartbeats of mules, the wings of enormous birds thrusting upward, the discarded world all ooze and steam and birthing creatures you couldn't possibly conceive. "Not in this life," he says. "Not even if you pile your craziest dreams one right on top of the other."

For months after he was taken away, I'd wake screaming, the sheets tangled and soaked with sweat, and my bedroom detached and floating sideways away from the house, above the backyards of neighbors we never had. But since I arrived I've been sleeping okay on the floor mattress, my dad's low snores a comfort. It's in large part how we're getting reacquainted: by certain familiar sounds rising and dying, the two of us side by side under the same roof again.

Still, it would definitely help buoy our moods if someone would call to hire us short notice. Or if we were at least having more fun while we waited throughout the mornings, and afternoons, and deeper into each evening. There's a portable black-and-white TV, but it's all scratch and static on the only channel he says sometimes comes in if you fiddle the rabbit ears just so. And no cards. No Monopoly or Clue, and naturally the nearest tenpin alley's two towns distant.

Don't get me wrong—I *do* like being here, how fast it cools down after sunset. But you can only watch the night shadows blur and brighten for so long as your eyes adjust and readjust to how nothing's like what it seemed in the daylight. That's why we're heading up to the landfill real soon. To break the monotony, the wear and tear on our nerves, being locked up for the most part. You'd think it'd be nonstop conversation with all this catching up to do, but these long and awkward silent stretches, they make me consider packing up and stealing away back home before the week's even completed.

My take is that for the sake of a good story, my dad exaggerated by a whole lot when he said, "You go cheap like they did on the vents, Sam Lee P., and it's the Big Bang all over again." I shrugged and he said, "No, I'm dead serious. Listen, it's the simple physics of matter decomposing. All that methane gas trapped and compacted and nowhere to go, and I'm thinking that you and me, we're the ones most at risk here, so what do you say we drive up there and lance that boil?"

A tricked-up impossible plot or not, it for sure beats hanging around here and listening to him talk in tongues. Like how someday eons from now the entire landfill might slide all the way south to Grand Rapids, where some filthy-rich doctor type or developer will buy it up and build a golf course or a hilltop mansion. Skylights and high ceilings and hallways that echo like train whistles.

I dry off with my same towel and get dressed, and I guess that my dad's finally done leafing through the pages of that same *Field & Stream*. For the time being anyhow. Unless he's calling me inside to point out for the umpteenth time an outboard he'd like to buy.

I don't mean to sound crass, or to imply that his growing checklist's a total fabrication. But piss in one hand and wish in the other and see which one fills first. That's what he used to say to me when he'd get frustrated, my mom asking, "Returnable bottle and can rescue? To benefit exactly who or what, Philly?" Which wasn't really a question, and the tone not at all charitable when another weekend scrap drive added up to little more than pocket change. Nonetheless, it tops what we've made thus far, and the odds appear better that a small-horse-power Mercury or Evinrude will erupt from some sunken river, the chrome propeller tearing through flame and moonlight at full bore right to this flimsy, half-corroded tin door.

"You all set?" he says, and next thing he's up and outside and rotating a flange on the truck's front-end assembly with a giant lock wrench. Then off come the set chains, like he's about to turn some secret danger loose on the world, the cab stripped bare except for the steering wheel and hydraulics, and when he climbs in and yanks back on one of the levers, the stump grinder wheezes slowly off the ground. Like an oversized brush-hog, or a minesweeper. Like something a long time dormant and, forced awake like this, angry and yawning and hungry for whatever gets in its way.

"Not bad for a rig left for dead," he says. He means the tilt-bed wrecker, which part by rescued part he's rebuilt, and which now features a rear wench that he claims is powerful enough to dredge up a bank safe or sunken car from the bottom muck beneath Brown Bridge. All I care is that the engine starts, and when it fires alive first try, he says, "Stick with me, Sam Lee P.," and he double-clutches, and within minutes the wrecker's bargelike and banging uphill through wave after grassy-thick wave tipped silver under the halo-glow of the moon and stars.

There's a flat spot on top, and when he stops and kills the head-lights I can see, in the afterimage of the dying filaments, blue mist rising all around us. But no foul air like at the rat dumps where we used to hunt, all those beady eyes liquid blind in the high beams, and my dad whispering, "That a boy. Okay, aim and squeeze." Up here's more like an overgrown fairway, treeless and quiet, and when I step down I can't feel anything breathing or seething around underneath.

For sure not wings, or swollen-up animal hearts, or anything trapped and still alive and thrashing to get loose. The bleached torsos of refrigerator doors, maybe, or the bones of old ladders, garbage bags bloated and flung like plastic lungs from open pickup beds. Stuff like that. Old sinks and busted brine barrels, and mangy carpeting yanked out of double-wides like the one where we used to live, all of us still together, and less than a half hour's drive from here. But fire-and-gas balls? Fine, right, but then someone explain the logic of my dad lighting up yet another cigarette.

"Stand back," he says. "Let's see how this brute roots and gorges."

There's not a stump in sight, of course. And why, I haven't a clue, but I flash on how grown-up lives turn out the way they do, my mom's framed diploma on the wall, and her, deaf to any consideration of my dad's remorse, or to him ever changing for the better. And the Big Bang, which we learned about in school last year, is where it all began, in absolute total darkness, before time itself exploded into this universe.

Dirt's erupting everywhere like scattershot, the augers biting so hard that the whole wrecker's shaking. And there's a tremor underfoot now, and the exploding tails of twin comets crisscrossing light-years from where my dad's hell-bent on trenching down to unearth some ghost or other. Some tiny dark heart that might pulse and glow in the grainy 3-D silhouette this night has offered up.

I cup my hands around my mouth and yell, "Dad, that's enough," but whatever he's just hit is lodged solid, metal screeching on metal so loud that I cover my ears and backpedal a few more feet. The sound is deafening, worse than the close-up wail of sirens.

Could be it's just an illusion, the wavering shadows and such, but the truck's front end appears to nosedive. He doesn't let up, and after another few minutes it tips farther forward. Beyond the windshield and all the way up to the doors, as if it's being towed underground, crowns of sparks churned skyward and showering back down all around him.

"Dad, shut it off. Shut it off, please, and get out of there before something blows," I say, but my throat's all stingers, swollen almost shut, and I'm screaming as if from those same nightmares my mom would wake me from, furious and cursing what my dad had done to himself and to us.

I close my eyes. It's all I can think to do, terrified that if I watch I'll witness him being swallowed into some bottomless cavern never to be seen or heard from again. Like magic, everything goes silent. I'm a little kid again, and I'm watching my mom's fingertips stroke my cheeks, my forehead. They're saying, "We'll be okay, you and me. You and me, Sam Lee," a rhyme I can't get enough of, how it pleads and pleads its simple singsong of love.

And how my dad's reciting it now, too, his version at least: "You okay, Sam Lee P.? Hey, you still with me?"

I don't answer, and he says, "Did you get a good look at that?" his voice low-pitched in the sudden calm, as if this is some huge and lucrative secret to be guarded. "Jesus, we got a demon on our hands, don't we now?"

"It sure works," I say, and he says back, "Work? Hell, it'd chew right through a pit grave of diamonds."

Diamonds, I think. And gold and silver, too, and to hear him tell it, come hell or high water, we'll get the wrecker and stump grinder unstuck first thing tomorrow morning, and continue to brainstorm our way to both fortune and fame. We're walking step for step through the knee-deep grass, and the northern lights flaring big time. He's sky-higher than ever on our prospects, and he says, "We'll make it happen, you hear me? We're in this for keeps, Sam Lee Penwaydon."

"Yes," I say, still disoriented but otherwise unafraid. And believing, almost—and most of all—that in the *final* tally, no matter how crazy, or how long it sometimes takes, a good father always gets it right.

A WOMAN
GONE MISSING

HER AGE IS THIRTY-THREE. Already twice divorced, though neither is the father of her teenage daughter, Trinity, who has opted to spend her junior year living with her biological dad four hours south in Kalamazoo. "Getting to know him better" is what she says.

His name is Bernard Sawyer. B-Saw back then, Vanessa's first serious high school boyfriend. Unlike her, he's a college graduate. A meteorologist. He sends up weather balloons to gather data and describes *his* failed marriage as a category-four. His vocation is his passion. Has been since grade school, and because he comes from money, and because he continues to take home a living wage, he's the one who paid for Trinity's braces—and, the day they came off, to have her model-perfect teeth bleached white as frostbite. Not to buy her off, because he's not like that. He's generous with Vanessa, too. Meaning that he has never one time, as far as she knows, slighted or maligned her in any way. To Trinity least of all. And yet, a metal-mouth no longer, this girl wants suddenly to shame the world with her beauty. Devour her mom's dour cautions about the thunderous, unrequited fantasies of love.

Knocked up on the high dive is how Vanessa might describe the night, the blatting slap of the pickup's tires as she and B-Saw crossed the narrow bridge, ignored the distant, intermittent heat lightning and the no trespassing signs. Then fishtailed up the steep two-track in four-wheel drive, no AC and the windows open. Hair blowing across her face and the humidity at 100 percent. Hotter than Hades, and the forecast going forward that called for more of the same. Tornado weather was what B-Saw said, and the drive seemed to her like forever, a sweaty six-pack of Rolling Rock between them on the shiny vinyl bench seat. Which, of course, is where they could have gotten laid a hundred times over. But they didn't, and, come hell or high water, they would never violate their commitment to each other to wait. No regrettable weak moments, though sixteen and horny they did everything but. A few times on the oversize living room couch in his parents' vacation cottage. Summer people who'd motor away in their pontoon, highballs in hand, as if to reward such responsible kids with a little space and privacy.

And still Vanessa and B-Saw stayed faithful to the plan. Had for the second summer in a row since they'd first met, and the planning became part of the foreplay. She, with the fairy-tale imagination, said, "In a tub of jasmine and white roses," though he opted for something less flowery, someplace dangerous and forbidden—and so, yes, *this* is where Vanessa goes, exactly where she stood high up on that same embankment while B-Saw peeled off her soaked-through tank top and cargo shorts, her bikini underpants, and hung them on a branch as if to dry in the nonexistent breeze, like laundry on a clothesline. Then *he* stripped, and together they descended, and waded naked into the subarctic spring-fed lake at midnight.

Great Hollow, it's called, and in the science of inexplicable natural phenomena, and against the base laws of latitude and longitude, and in the absence of any known thermal vein or current, the lake, even in deepest winter, refuses to freeze over.

Not withstanding that neither Vanessa nor B-Saw could see it, he swore the abandoned tower rig lay straight ahead, the surface shadowless and flat-calm and silvery, trout colored. Whatever had been mined down there he didn't know. Possibly diamonds, he said, a lie she liked, and she pointed at the sky alive with millions and millions of glittering stars. He'd memorized their names, which ones formed which constellations—Swan, Bear, the Three Guides, and the Three Hunters. A sixty-minute swimmer, she'd already started to shiver as they breast-stroked side by side through pockets of water so frigid she could feel her calves and thighs tighten and throb, her lungs collapsing like a bellows, teeth chattering. It was too cold even to pee, and she almost said, "Help me." She almost said, "We can't, we've got to turn back," but there it was, like something out of *War of the Worlds* looming above them in the moonlight.

They treaded water, craned their necks heavenward, with the safe and commonplace queen-size or truck seat or couch suddenly drifting away like images from another galaxy. She'd begun to lose her coordination when she grabbed hold of the ladder, and as she climbed slowly upward her knuckles appeared blue on the corroded wrought-iron rungs. She wondered if it was mist or smoke or the steam from their human bodies rising all around them, rising above the gold-tipped tops of the shoreline trees the higher she got, with B-Saw so close she could feel his breath warm on her backside.

At some point he'd let go of the sealed condom, and no, she'd never exactly committed to the pill. Not that she meant to get pregnant, but like the two last survivors on a sinking ocean liner they did it anyway, in a crow's nest seventy-five feet in the sky. They did it quickly, standing, cheek to cheek, her legs barely apart, and each vertebra in her back pressing hard against what must have been a mast or a flagpole. A bride and groom, she later thought, slow-dancing nude on a wedding cake, though already long vanished was any happily-ever-after, the marriage that never was.

And gone, too, is Vanessa's daughter, who packed up her entire room, closet, and bureau drawers. Everything but the full-length bedroom mirror, in front of which, before exiting, she paused, cocked her hip, and said, "There," as if imagining herself in fishnet and high heels, the starlet of some banned bootleg music video.

CLINTON STYLES—the man Vanessa did marry. And although he kept the volume low, the videos he owned and watched were violent: *Full Metal Jacket, A Clockwork Orange, Reservoir Dogs.* "All four and five stars," he argued, "classic flicks"—which meant nothing to her, and she asked him to please *not* set that mousetrap under the heating grate by the TV anymore. It frightened her whenever it snapped and rattled and ruined whatever show she was watching. Romantic comedies mostly, where people not so unlike her almost always turned out okay.

But one evening during dinner, barely four months after they'd tied the knot, Clinton said, "No, it's a lot of different things." He'd *wanted* to give the marriage his all. Believed against the odds that it could work its magic, but "What," he said, "in hell's name was I thinking?" Meaning their seven-year difference in age and how little they knew each other, the whirlwind of it all. Meaning stepfatherhood. Meaning diapers and diaper bags that no amount of Tide ever seemed to get completely white and clean-smelling. The baby colicky and wailing, and him being relegated to smoking his Lucky Strikes outside no matter the time or the weather, as if she and Trinity had taken up sides against him. Without asking, Vanessa had emptied the cigarette butts and sponged clean the ashtrays and stored them away, out of sight. As for the oval burn scars on the Formica countertop, there was precious little she could do, other than to point each one out as a house fire waiting to happen, and their security deposit already gone up in flames.

"Go ahead. Keep this up," he said. He said, "Fuck it," maybe he'd just as soon trade in the whole goddamn loused-up deal for a bottle of muscatel, a Motel 6, and a screamer to pile-drive and pay for and be done with. The occasional fist through a plasterboard wall.

But that wasn't Clinton at all; it was pure frustration talking, and she'd whisper in bed, "Shh, you'll wake the baby," and she'd slip out to the sleeping porch the instant he rolled off her and started to snore. Better this, she thought, than to quit the marriage cold and go live with her mother, the worst of the worst of all possible options. And there were, after all, nights on the porch when it smelled like rain, and moths pinged like moist cotton balls against the screens. Her complexion was perfect then, and her breasts still twice their normal size, her stretch marks beginning to disappear. To mention nothing of her lips, and those long, upcurled eyelashes, the natural dance of her waist and hips when she walked.

Her long-term goal was to homeschool herself, develop study skills like B-Saw had, and get her GED, perhaps at some point take night classes and graduate with a nursing or pharmacy degree from the community college in Traverse City. After all, how difficult could it be to count pills into those opaque orange containers, like the ones her mother lined up on the shelves of their medicine cabinet? But first things first, she thought, and promised herself that starting the very next day she'd stop eating peanut butter and raspberry preserves straight from the jars with a spoon. That didn't happen, and Clinton joked, "Tamper-proof lids. That's the ticket." They didn't yet own a bathroom scale, but it wasn't easy to miss that she'd already started to put on weight. He smiled. "Baby fat," he said.

Before she'd ever met Clinton she'd concluded, "Why not?" to a start-up, rebound romance, after B-Saw, who drove up three different times to see her, said, "Please, Vanessa. Listen to me," but she wouldn't, her decision as decisive and final and as contrary as his. A test of wills. "And, in case you're interested," she said, "the baby's due date is May. Possibly even on Mother's Day."

She acknowledged *his* position, said yes, they'd screwed up, a mess of their own making. "I admit it, okay?" she said. His parents had blamed her as if she'd set out to trap their son, this wild and headstrong girl who refused to come to her senses. But B-Saw never encouraged that, never poor-mouthed or backstabbed. It was always *we*, always *us*. And never any tirades or taunts, and not one time during her early term did he mention the A-word. It was her mother who said, "There *are* no free abortion clinics, not here in Mancelona there aren't. But somewhere. Believe me, you have it and you'll never, for as long as you live, feel young like this again. Never."

As if for one single solitary second Vanessa had conceived of such a cowardly, unthinkable act. She'd relocate, but not for that, to Frankfort, a tourist town where maybe a young pregnant girl waiting tables could pull down decent tips. She'd been there once and liked it, the beach and the break-wall, the public park. But no matter where or what, she'd have the baby. And not only wouldn't she put it up for adoption, she'd do a way better job of raising her child than her mother ever did, which wasn't saying a whole lot.

And Clinton Styles, hadn't he recently completed a stint in the navy, his ambition to someday become a merchant marine? That's what he claimed, on Lake Michigan or Lake Superior, and his favorite song Gordon Lightfoot's "The Wreck of the Edmund Fitzgerald," a few verses of which he sang to her. He'd recently moved from Bad Axe to Frankfort to be closer to a maritime academy, though he hadn't yet gotten around to submitting his application.

He was 6' 2", eyes blue-gray like a husky's, his car a bright-red, high-mileage Chevy Nova, insured by State Farm. Plus he'd handed her a bank passbook with more deposits than withdrawals. Collateral, she thought, and his voice just disarming enough to convince her that a life together need not be — and as he promised it wouldn't be — all mongoose and cobra.

As for his gig back then, rotating a two-sided octagonal sign on a pole — STOP and SLOW — and the diesel and tar fumes so strong he'd arrive back home to the motor court with fewer and fewer brain cells under his yellow hard hat? "Mindless," he said. "One-armed," and he'd swivel his wrist one way and then back the other. "Totally rinky-dink and so boring." But she shouldn't lose heart, it was only temporary. True or not, it constituted for Vanessa the closest thing available to a protected and halfway stable life, a decent enough paycheck every two weeks, a roof over her infant daughter's head, and bread on the table, a Frigidaire that stayed cold. And, admittedly, a life with someone she maybe didn't entirely know and love, but someday she might, and she at least trusted him to watch Trinity when Vanessa showered and shaved her underarms and legs, a towel twirled around her head like a turban.

In his defense, Clinton was *not* a wife-beater, a thief, or a cheat, or an ugly drunk who'd say, "What the fuck are *you* looking at?" and then hurl himself across the dinner table to scream in her face. And no window curtains blown back from a thrown boot or a gunshot blast. She'd seen enough of that in her growing up, before her father was arrested and convicted of crimes both petty and serious, and eventually sentenced away.

And there were, in fact, for as long as the marriage lasted, calm and companionable quiet stretches, TV shows they agreed on and Trinity asleep in her crib, most likely dreaming good dreams. It's fair to say that on certain days, whatever their future held seemed no more and no less haunted for them than it did for anyone else.

They'd met, for god's sake, she and Clinton, at the public library, where Vanessa was shelving books from a cart. One of her two part-time jobs, and Trinity like a papoose on her mother's back, the best-behaved baby ever. Poster child. Fat cheeks, and her hair shiny-black and spiked like a Mohawk. A magnet for lonely men, who stopped and whispered, "She's so beautiful. Is she yours?" Sometimes they'd take her tiny pink hand between their thumb and index finger, and one time an older guy with a misshapen smile and overbite tucked a smudgy phone number into Trinity's squeezed palm. Whenever Vanessa turned around, these strangers always seemed stunned that she wasn't Ottawa or Chippewa, wasn't from the reservation. Stunned, too, by how young she was, like someone they might have seen not all that long ago playing hopscotch or jumping rope on a sidewalk.

What Clinton Styles asked about when he said, "Excuse me" was a reading recommendation. "Science fiction, I guess?" he said. "Or a good Western? Nothing too heavy." Back then she hadn't been much of a reader, so she simply shrugged and, using both hands, offered him the book she'd just lifted from her stack and was about to shelve. Its title, *The Elegant Universe*.

And so, no, for her it wasn't love at first sight, but he was polite, not unattractive. A mask, her mother said. "Don't kid yourself, they've all got issues and needs. Go slow—he's been around, unlike you," she cautioned. Vanessa agreed, even under such desperate circumstances, that what she really needed was a live-in, a roommate, not a husband, and what she *should* have said when he proposed was, "Okay, yes, I will. I accept, but remember, no sex after marriage."

They kept the wedding simple, with a justice of the peace and the ceremony absent any frills or pageantry. No best man, no maid of honor, and the ring sized, she thought, to fit her pinkie or to wear on a chain around her neck. Not so much as a walk-through rehearsal. They simply showed up at the courthouse casually dressed. (A bridal registry, Vanessa concluded, must be where couples like them paid for the service.) And her mother, weeks after the fact, when Vanessa described it, said, "What'd you expect on a mercy rescue? Complete strangers throwing rice? A reception of lobster ravioli and corked champagne? A honeymoon at the Mall of America?"

And the bigger question, "Do you, Vanessa, take this man?"—who one year later to the day, on the eve of their first wedding anniversary, left her the Nova, the key and the title, and the remaining twelve payments. Either that or sell the car for whatever she could get. Plus he'd signed a check for the next two months' rent. Then he hitchhiked downstate and took a ferry from Ludington to Milwaukee, Wisconsin. The note he left also said, "From there, wherever it leads." It said, "No regrets. It's simply where we left off." It said, "And remember, never spoil the ending." Just like that. Broosh. Gone, and never a single postcard to follow.

That night the trees out back whipsawed, and although there was no damage from the falling limbs, gale-force winds ripped shingles from the roof. It was already a week after Thanksgiving, and she needed to baste and cook that thawed, bruised-looking tom in the tinfoil turkey tray before he spoiled. One hundred and eighty degrees for the breast, one-twenty for the thighs is what that gourmet TV chef had recommended. Sure. But her days were still hand-to-mouth, and she hadn't budgeted for a cookbook or a meat thermometer or even an inexpensive apron, so how, with an oven she'd barely used, and a husband who'd ditched out on her, did someone manage that?

"A Mexican divorce in goddamn Michigan," her mother would have said. "A blessing that the power went out during the storm — that turkey's just one less thing to fail at and beat yourself up about. And for what?" Another lost someone to feel sorry enough to bail her out? Serves her right. After all, Vanessa could have gone home for the holiday. Hadn't she gotten her driver's license? She had a car, a safety seat for the baby, and so why *hadn't* she simply picked up the phone and dialed?

Every now and again she does. She closes her eyes, and breathes deeply, and summons the nerve. Her mother's fifty-two. She lives alone in that same house where Vanessa was raised, and sometimes, like now, while sipping a glass of Diet Rite and vodka at twilight, Vanessa will close her eyes and, against her will and better judgment, she'll go there again.

THERE *HE* IS, her father, facedown in the backyard of 1050 Willow Road, his fists balled, and Vanessa's mother strangle-voiced and saying, "Christ Almighty." Her throat is rubbed red as rhubarb, her left eye half-closed and swollen, her brutal dye job grown out a full inch at the roots. It's not the first time he's done this, but she says, "Accidents happen, you'll see. Just leave him alone, leave him be. He'll make his way inside on his own." She says, "Sweet Jesus," as she lights a cigarette, her red fingernails chipped and her hands trembling. "Just another goddamn day in Paradise." She says it in gulps, like she should be deep breathing into a paper bag.

But by morning he's nowhere in the house or on the property. Not that they can detect, though it's all junked up out there, a regular dump, and could be he's asleep in the back seat on any one of those half-dozen beaters. Wrecks he's towed in over time, hoods popped, and the smashed windshields infused with what look to Vanessa in the early light like giant, silvery-blue spider webs. Convex and oval-shaped, what she understands in retrospect to be the perfect head-on impressions of anonymous human skulls and faces.

She has just turned eight, and she wonders why the prior evening's brightest star has survived so long into the daylight. Her mother hasn't a clue, and Margie, Baby Doll is what he calls her when he finally *does* reappear after two days, hangdog and hungover as usual, and although his hands stay shaky on her hipbones, he says, "Truce." Says, "We're good. You'll see. I promise we'll figure this out."

But that summer nobody's good with much of anything. Delinquent mortgage payments, a rust-ravaged car that even he can't start anymore. A single offhand, mistimed remark and tempers flare like hay fires, so much meanness and shouting that Vanessa has to cover her ears and hum while the ground shifts and tilts around her. Because he's been fired and laid off and fired again, he's recruited her to assist him in his new job so he can spoil her rotten, buy her everything she wants. Root beer floats and a Cabbage Patch doll, a bicycle pump so he can inflate her flat rear tire.

"How?" she asks. "And when?" and he brushes her bangs back from her forehead and says, "Come on, I'll show you. Hop in."

She's not supposed to ride in the truck, a flatbed with no passenger-side seat belt, but her mother, like always after a drag-down, is napping. She's swallowed those pills again. She's dead to the world, and she'll be conked for a long while and groggy and silent when she wakes, her eye already turned a sallow yellow and green.

And yes, that loose front tooth Vanessa pushes on with her tongue tip both hurts and soothes, and her father says, "Now remember, you just stand there, right next to me, and act like you're about to cry." She hardly ever cries anymore, and, in that 7-Eleven, the E-Z-Mart, and the Tastee Freez a couple of towns over, she listens to him as he harangues each confused and apologetic cashier. "And the purchase price was how much? All right then. Here, go ahead, count it yourself," he says, and hands back the bills. "That's correct, you short-changed me," and even Vanessa, an eyewitness to his every sleight of hand, cannot detect how he does it, like a card shark or magician.

"Bingo," he says on the ride home, "easy as that." He says, "Now we're getting somewhere," but the money's mostly lost to the booze and cigarettes, and a week later he strips a house, foreclosed and standing empty, of its fancy crown molding and mahogany doors. What he calls salvage and scrap, serious profit, but his quick resale estimates are so far under that he needs another beer and a shot, another Pall Mall, something to dull the great dismay that is theirs ongoing.

Needs, on yet another caper, for Vanessa to scale a drainpipe or trellis to a second-story balcony or porch. To sneak inside and down the stairs to unlock the rear slider. "That's it," he says, "good work," before the more serious looting ensues in bedrooms and dens. Eventually this ends, first with his arrest, then the guilty as charged and, as a multiple repeat offender, no less than fifteen years in a federal penitentiary. Before he is led away in handcuffs and asked by the judge if he has anything to say to the court, he nods, shrugs. He is already standing. He says, as if it were a last request, "Just wondering if anyone here's got a smoke they can spare for the dead?"

SOMETIMES VANESSA CAN HEAR her mother's noisy inhale, the cigarette paper crackling through the phone lines like distant radio static. It's been two and a half decades since Vanessa last saw or spoke to her father. Trinity knows next to nothing about him. "I was eight when he left," Vanessa tells her. "I hardly remember him at all."

"Eight?" Trinity thinks, knowing *she* remembers plenty from when she was that age, which instantly invalidates the amnesia of her mother's past. Aloud she says, "Maybe someday...," but she doesn't finish, as if to solve the mystery or cover up might distance the two of them even further. Trinity just offers her icy, unblinking stare and adds, "Dad, he tells me everything."

She favors him in looks, too, same shiny black hair, same straight nose, and that sudden slow-motion chewing whenever a dinner conversation stalls or loses its bearings. It's no wonder she opts for the Sawyer side of the family.

"They're educated. They're nice," Trinity says. "They don't play Risk or Go Fish all night to kill time. Talk to me. And they travel everywhere. They go on cruises and have their leaves blown and they don't live a million miles out in the boonies."

To hear her daughter talk, obviously it means nothing that her maternal grandmother squeezed Vanessa's hand throughout the entire eight hours of that interminable labor. Nor do those picture books Vanessa had saved, and that mobile of black-and-white sandhill cranes she made that danced in the air currents above Trinity's crib mean anything. The girl has threatened to legally change her name from Lavanway to Sawyer when she turns eighteen. She says that her *other* grandparents have two Siamese cats that sleep right on the bed with her and purr and purr whenever she visits.

The closest thing to a pet that Vanessa ever had were nasty, beady-eyed minks that her father bred and raised in cages behind their house. They frightened her, captive wild creatures with their fanglike incisors and high-shrieking midnight wails into the snow or the wind. Into whatever disease and neglect finally killed every last one of them, their pelts ratty and dull and worthless. Vanessa has never admitted as much, but despite her banishment, she'd always hoped that after their grandchild was born the Sawyers would relinquish such a selfish, and superior, and unreasonable stance against her.

They never did, as if the score they needed to settle was with time itself, and what Vanessa has wanted to tell them was, no one lives long enough for that. Although she's got nothing to answer for anymore, she'll be forever unwelcome there, and so instead she diets down a few pounds and feels better. Almost like herself again, she laces up her cross-trainers and runs at night whenever Trinity's away, and when sleep, that sweet and distant rain, falls so rarely.

It's why Vanessa is wide-awake and out the back door, down the steps, the neighborhood quiet, the windows dark everywhere. Ready, set, go. And in her rush to get away, she doesn't even bother to stretch, her legs churning as she veers across backyard lawns, the freshly mown grass lush and oddly fragrant. She knows this route so well she can do it with her eyes closed, and sometimes for almost half a minute she does, blind to all those security spots snapping on, one after the other, and lighting up the distance behind her as she goes.

Why? Because this is the hour of the wolf, and so even when she stops she continues to run in place. Like now, under a full moon, where the slide and the jungle gym and the bars of the swing set shine like platinum, and her heart racing and racing as if she's been chased. But there's no one around. Just a lazy waterspout, and a fountain where lonely daytimers toss nickels and dimes and quarters. What *she* wishes for is a body better shaped to carry the weight of her drooping ass—bringing up the rear, as her second husband, half-drunk in the sack, liked to say. But he's long gone, too, so X the ex and, if need be, she'll hump it until dawn in every conceivable roundabout, zigzagging direction home just to be rid of him in her mind.

Since divorce number two she's allowed only a handful of men to follow her inside, though almost never beyond the kitchen or living room. Ironically, and in Trinity's absence, she's decided to quit them, too, their come-ons and promises, which, calculated in time and regret, have cost her plenty.

The prenup, as well—but at least, and without a court battle, she's ended up with the house. Not rented—owned. *Her* place and everything up to code, wiring and plumbing, with the driveway recently resurfaced. A safe neighborhood and a manageable mortgage, and just last month she took that second pillow off the bed, a symbolic act, and invoked the mercy rule on dating.

"I'm done," she said to Trinity on the phone. Trinity, who refused to be introduced to any and all future men of the house, but nonetheless hurried downstairs whenever the doorbell rang, and stood there stone-faced. Said nothing. Gave them long, dark looks, a silent send-off to wherever her mother was headed: to a movie or dinner or the bar at the bowling alley. At worst, and depending on whether she'd had a second Bloody Mary or screwdriver, a make-out session in the guy's car parked a block or two away. But even then, Vanessa was always back before ten, her self-imposed, romance-killing curfew.

All she really wants in the end is for her daughter to come back home. Re-enroll at her old school and visit her father every other weekend, like she'd been doing for the past couple of years. Only once a month before that, and before that hardly ever.

Factor in Vanessa's recent raise as floor manager at Old World Gifts and Furnishings, and she's finally had a satellite dish installed. With the remote Trinity could now flip through hundreds of channels and watch whatever she wants. Watch B-Saw, in fact, on that all-weather station as he arcs his arms like a god. As if *he's* compelling those sped-up incandescent radar blobs that swirl across the new flat-screen, west to east, across the vastness of all those places Vanessa has never been.

And worse, she tunes in and way more often than she probably should. She's learned the language: temperature bands, snow thunder, wind-chill factors, jet streams and supercells, the weekly almanac. Sunset and sunrise. But the segment she likes best by far is called "*Show Me a Glory.*" It's where viewers send in photographs of sundogs or the Belt of Venus, or that rare moonbow captured last week in the sky above Sweet Lips, Tennessee. All these from people who, unlike Vanessa, own telescopes and fancy-ass cameras and keep a careful watch on the world.

Moreover, she actually fantasizes about sending in that blurry Polaroid she's saved of her and B-Saw from their junior year. They're standing on the abandoned soccer field of her old high school, and he's hugging her from behind. He'd set the camera on a tripod, on a five-second delay. They're in love. They're facing into the afternoon light, and they're almost glowing, radiant against that background of random, ordinary clouds on an ordinary late-summer afternoon in 1985. If she were to follow through, she halfway believes, for old time's sake—for that moment when the shutter clicked and that already developing snapshot slid toward them—that he might reach out like he did then, and show it, along with those sprites and elves and blue jets: the tiny, bright, emerald-colored auroras trapped inside raindrops that illuminate the nighttime ground as they spiral and fall.

EVERYTHING, Vanessa concludes, is more or less what it seems. And more so all the time, year in and year out. Right, the mercury rises, the mercury falls—like the seasons, and already it's February again, the snowbanks piled high, and the county plows tearing by all growl and sparks and flashing orange beacons. She's invested in quality snow tires. Emergency provisions such as road flares and extra matches, Mars bars and a Hudson Bay blanket stored in the trunk. Jumper cables. But on a night like this, and the storm predicted to worsen, who's going anywhere?

What she hears from Trinity is need-to-know only. Thinly coded signals and dispatches. The girl is pulling down good grades for the first time ever, an A in chemistry, a B+ in AP English. She's on a mission of merit and discovery, her father all over again. She's got a sun lamp by her desk, she says, and recommends that Vanessa get one, too. "Especially up where you are," she says, as if it's the cure for all her mother's longings and moods.

About Trinity's bedroom being repainted a lighter blue, and the new TV and satellite dish, her daughter says, "Maybe over spring break, okay?" But that followed immediately with something about a getaway vacation to the Grand Canyon. "The Southwest," she says, as if Vanessa had never opened a Rand McNally or spun a globe in grade school. As if she has never imagined anyplace other than the great white nothingness of winter on the forty-fifth parallel.

Maybe now is the perfect time, Vanessa thinks, for a mother-daughter road trip. Or possibly all three of them could travel together.

Rent an RV, chart a course, and end each day in a different state park campsite along the rims of famous canyons and rivers and lakes, before it's too late.

But it's B-Saw talking first thing once he gets on the phone. He's all business, friendly as always—but distant, and so mostly she only half-listens and drifts. Her feet are tucked under her on the couch, and she's poured a shot of whiskey into her coffee. Taster's Choice. It's become a ritual—the aroma, the sheen of the steaming crystals. She knows, by the time she finishes her second cup, she'll be good to go. She'll close her eyes, lean back, navigate by dogsled if need be, across a landscape so white and flat that she might in fact be dreaming.

"Mush," she says after she hangs up. She almost laughs, and yet, within minutes, she can almost hear the dogs huffing and howling under the icy-blue crescent of the moon outside her window. But no, she does not walk out onto the porch and down the steps into the yard in her nightgown. Instead, and because she makes this slow trek down the hallway to her bed, and sets her alarm clock for work, there will be no freezing to death, no lost fingers or toes in this story. It's hers. It's ongoing, and so she'll go there, too, and it goes like this.

HERE'S HOW
IT WORKS

MY HALF BROTHER COLE INSISTS that our mom only dates former inmates, and that he can bull's-eye, give or take, the length of their incarcerations. "Yeah, right," I say. "A year for every second they stare at us while Mom emcees the intros."

"No," he says. "Not even close." And then he turns sullen and silent. For as far back as I can remember he's reacted like this, hardwired to hate them, to run them off.

He's eleven, and impossible to reason with, and way too smart for his own good. Already he reads at a twelfth-grade level, and uses more big words than most adults. *Especially* our mom's male companions, at least according to him—"the enemy," as he calls them, "the criminals," and mimics the contortions their lips sometimes make before they can even say, "Hi," or "How goes it?" or "What's the good word, guys?" He refuses to shake their hands, laser-eyes them and walks away before our mom can so much as utter their names.

Stand-ins. Here and gone, and Cole, on the off chance that our real dads might someday come back to check-see if we actually exist, holding firm. Even though our mom's made clear about a gazillion times, "You've lived at the same address for how long? Virtually your entire lives, is that correct? Then trust me, anyone wants to find you boys, you're not all that difficult to locate."

Could be, but I'll give Cole this: if they ever do stop by there'll be no mistaking us, one from the other, given that we bear not the slightest resemblance to each other. Flipsides of the same coin is what our mom maintains. Me happy-go-lucky enough, but Cole, he's wound pretty tight, a nervous wreck of a kid, suspicious and distrustful of almost everyone who isn't us.

Physically, I stand five-foot-nine-and-a-half. Way tall for my age, wiry, wide-shouldered, and almost three years Cole's elder, and a high school freshman starting this September. Hazel and honeycomb, that's me—blond curls, deep bronze tan. Plus I'm a whiz at math, at numbers, a subject he loathes, and how he plans to survive the bus ride each early morning and late afternoon in my absence is what worries me most. With his nose in a book and huddled up right behind the bus driver, I guess. And all the while silently cursing those dipshits Johnny Ozmott and Donnie Bembeneck every time a spongy spitball whacks the back of his head.

He's pale-skinned like someone allergic to the sun—his face and arms and throat, the back of his neck, all white, even in late summer. Pudgy and nearsighted he wears these thick-lensed glasses that make him appear popeyed, his hair jet-black and combed into a pompadour like Elvis. "Maybe *he's* your old man," I joked first time I saw the do, though our mom made clear if so there'd be one hell of a paternity suit pending. Not to mention Cole's vocal chords, which, when he turns hyper, register that same wheezing frequency of the paneling being pried loose from our wall, the delaminating remnants still stacked in a warped pile on the living room floor. Bare studs and the ancient, snakelike wiring exposed. One more renovation terminated, as he says, "Until Mom hooks up and hangs with another handyman long enough to give the place a makeover."

"So?" I tell him. "Whatever needs fixing around here, and if someone offers to help? It's no big deal."

"Maybe not to you," he says, and I remind him yet again that she's all but given up on men lately, or them on her. Not that she's aged out or anything. After all, she's only thirty-two, slender and attractive, an athlete's calves from those endless hours on her feet. And although almost no one gets to see her do it, when she applies her deodorant, arms raised, she looks like a ballet dancer. Great smile, too. That is, if she's not scowling or in tears. Or, at her worst, hyperventilating into a paper bag. Even so, it's a rare occasion anymore to lay eyes on the same guy more than once or twice, which is why these different projects are undertaken and left in an even bigger mess.

"Happy now?" she always says after they've bugged out, and, at her wits end, she'll lead us outside and into the garage and point in frustration at the hand and power tools that we suspect one of our dads might have abandoned before *he* vacated.

We busy ourselves by palming wood planers and drill handles while she lights into us, and it's not until after she storms out that Cole glances up and takes aim at where she's been standing, and, using both hands, squeezes the chrome trigger of the staple gun. Blanks, but still, and as to whose dad the tools might belong to? The more Cole presses, the less she's apt to tell us.

"Why keep bringing this up? Why does it frigging matter so much?" she wants to know. *She's* the responsible parent. The *only* parent, and she threatens that she'll teach herself carpentry skills enough to bolt the mismatched furniture to the goddamn floor. And this: In just the right light when she comes unglued, her pupils turn silver as nail heads.

Not that anything's been repossessed, at least not so far. And unlike Cole, who flunked phys ed for failing to complete a single pull-up, I'll kick anyone's duff who shows up around here hell-bent on taking what's rightfully ours. And that includes any court-ordered intervention to snatch us kids. Like we're foster or wayward or orphaned, the unwanteds who go unfed. "More like kidnapped," Cole says, "and dumped out here in the middle of nowhere. In a place that time forgot."

He gets that stuff from those novels he reads, and I tell him, "Hey, listen to me for once, okay? We're here and we're fine and nobody's taking anyone or anything. Just let 'em try," I say, and ball both fists, and it's at tensed-up times like these, when our mom's most upset, that she's likely to let something slip. To choke up and hug me, the man of the house, and say, "Yes, you were born to it. It's in your blood, Glen."

As if distilled from a thousand hypotheticals, *my* dad might have been a bodyguard or a bouncer. Or better still, a cage fighter. "You know, against retired circus bears and kangaroos," is what I once told Cole, but on the subject of fathers I need to be real careful, given how he freaks when I wisecrack or make shit up. He says that our dads are betrayers enough, frauds. And that our mom, consciously or not, alters or flat-out lies about previously established facts. Like having moved here from Cleveland, except that the license plate nailed to the back wall of the garage says LIVE FREE OR DIE. Nineteen eighty, according to the expiration sticker, a full two years before Cole was born.

"That's New Hampshire," he says, "not Ohio." And she conveniently draws a total blank every time she mixes herself a second White Russian. I'm convinced she does it on purpose, charting a course so misleading that we don't stand a snowball's chance of ever finding our way to them, our phantom fathers. Like they're nothing more than figments that torment our overactive imaginations.

Currently, she bartends four nights a week at the Seven Monks Bar & Grill out on Route 35, a straight shot between Ishpeming and Palmer. Nine-hour shifts, and it's rare that she pulls into our driveway much before midnight. She claims it's only temporary, a regular paycheck while she narrows her list of other options. Nursing's one that's come up. Or a veterinarian's assistant, which makes us suspicious, given that she's got this wicked boomerang-shaped scar that curves from her right heel to her instep—from a dog attack when she was half Cole's age. Furthermore, we've never owned a pet of any kind other than tropical fish, so we're not so sure where she's headed with that fantasy anyhow. Her motto: "Shit luck is shit luck, plain and simple." And we've endured our fair share, but if we study hard and stay out of trouble, we'll up the odds that it'll skip a generation.

Her birth name is Pride, first name Bridgett, and Pride, that's what we go by, too. Her advice to us is that sometimes it pays, like it or not, to just shut our yaps and swallow hard. I get what she's saying, though it sounds to me more a built-in excuse for why, after almost three years, she's still employed where she's at, and possibly even likes it. I mean it's the only time she puts on lipstick, shiny and bright, like red foil, painted fingernails to match. Along with too much eyeliner, and with that black leotard top tucked into her skintight jeans, Cole argues she's right at home there, and in no danger of being mistaken for *anyone's* mom, single or otherwise. He says, "As far as jobs go, where, and how else would she meet so many losers?"

He's got in mind to be a science-fiction writer when he grows up. Other places, other worlds, light-years distant from these parts.

And me? I've got a crush on Eileen Lickteig, who I witnessed perform a slow-motion splits, hands on her hips, right on top of Mr. Pelizzari's coffin-sized desk mere seconds before he shuffled back into the classroom, where everyone sat silent and stunned. Except for Eileen, who leaned nonchalantly back in her seat, legs crossed, and lipped the tip of her shiny, strawberry-blond braid.

I've got it bad for her, the short skirts she wears, and I calculate that by the time I get my driver's license I'll have saved up enough hard cash to afford a high-mileage muscle car at Ware's Auto Auction. A Dodge Charger or Plymouth Fury. A convertible, a V-8 with dual exhausts. I'll invite her to accompany me, on a dare, to the long-abandoned copper mine, where, before we moved here, a meteor dead-centered and torpedoed downward, transforming it into what now looks more like a quarry, minus a Tarzan swing. For one thing, the only standing trees are as branchless as telephone poles or pilings, and the petrified trunks sound like distant church bells when you tap-tap them with your knuckles.

We never wear gloves or jackets, but catch this: Even in late July the water is so frigid that the surrounding air temperature plummets by thirty-five degrees. You can see your breath, and, on clear nights, comets' tails burn out right above us in disappearing arcs like tracer fire.

Our mom claims that it's haunted and dangerous, toxic, probably radioactive. Thus the price of our rent-to-own cheap-assed matchbox, as she calls it, which she took sight unseen. Seven acres and no neighbors and a graveyard of rusted-out tin cans and tires as bald and foreign as blacktop. I've walked the property lines, the rear boundary barbed-wired, and beyond that, the endless fields of cow corn and soy. And, last but not least, the place is located far from anywhere she'd ever before been. "Sounds to me like someone on the run," Cole says. "Like someone looking to hide something big."

She's mentioned the EPA—whatever that is—and says a blight like what happened at the mine would've been, anywhere else, cleaned up or condemned and filled in, every last underground shaft and vein and crevice. That it's a death pit.

She's not alone. Rumor has it that two local wreckers spooled out almost three hundred feet of cable before their drag hooks finally snagged a rear bumper. And that it took until late the next afternoon to hoist the vehicle topside. Both doors and trunk caved in and what looked like waterfalls gushing from all four windows, and the bodies of those two teenage lovers never, to this day, recovered.

Naturally, we're forbidden to bike those three or four miles, but right there's the power of boredom, given that we make at least a few test runs each week. Cole has trouble shifting gears on his three-speed, a secondhand Schwinn like mine. It doesn't take long before he's sucking air. He dismounts and, flatfooted, pushes uphill to that next flat stretch where he gets back on. No chain guard, and his unlaced high-tops like an accident waiting to happen.

"Tie your right one at least," I tell him, and to roll up those frayed and baggy pant cuffs, hand-me-downs I've long ago outgrown. But really, it's like talking to a deaf kid, and I think, *Fine*, and pump harder, barreling ahead. He's never once wiped out or called for me to slow down, knowing that I'll eventually figure-eight back to him so we can pedal, side by side, those final fifteen or twenty feet right up to the cliffside's foot-long overhang.

No DANGER or NO TRESSPASSING signs, nothing secured or fenced off. Plus there's an overturned aluminum rowboat by the shallow end but no oars that we've been able to locate.

"Maybe it floated up when the mine erupted," Cole says. "Maybe someone down there was saved."

That's typical Cole, and I tell him, "More like duck hunters," and I've since watched the occasional pair of goldeneyes whistle by overhead, but nothing ever lands, and never a single rising fish. Could be the water's too cold and deep, but not so wide that someone with a decent spinning rod and reel couldn't power cast a Daredevil halfway across.

If we time it right and arrive just before dusk, we can watch the spokes of our front wheels frost over, our fingers squeezing the handbrakes flat to the rubber grips, our heels dug into the hardpack. "It's *not* haunted," Cole says. "Home's haunted. School, too. This, uh-uh. It's electromagnetic. And it's all ours." But to do what with was my first question, and I still haven't gotten used to that bitter metallic taste, and the weird pressure under our tongues whenever we talk for more than a few minutes.

All that matters is that he waits all day for our mom to go to work so we can trek up, just the two of us. A scaled-down northern Michigan version of the Bermuda Triangle is his take. And, to prove it true, the last thing before we leave the house he'll wind his fancy diver's wristwatch, a combination Christmas and birthday present from our mom, and synchronize it with the digital stove clock. "Check," he'll say, and I'll nod and roll my eyes, but without fail when we get back home the times are always off—minimum—by half an hour.

"You turned it back," I said after our initial run, but I've since witnessed his glow-in-the-dark compass needle spin in slow, wavering half circles whenever he holds it at arm's length out over the abyss. His vocabulary includes terms like photons and volts and frequen cies. Currents. Radio waves and refractions, vortexes—and sometimes when the mist swirls and spirals in bands of greenish, phosphorescent light, I'll concede that *Ghostbusters*, his all-time favorite flick, might not constitute such a screwball premise after all.

I've seen bats strobe over and disappear. I've watched steam rise in full darkness like dragon's breath and swallow the beams of our flashlights. I've flinted a cigarette lifted from our mom's purse and watched the match flame spark like a fuse, the inhaled smoke burning like dry ice in my lungs. And although we haven't yet performed the experiment, I half-believe Cole that squeezing an eyedropper's worth of whatever's down there into the aquarium would make our last two surviving angelfish glow luminous like the moon and spawn a new species with oversize eyes and brains and wings the color of platinum.

Anyway, here's how it works: Our mom trusts me to watch over Cole, and in payment she deposits half her tip change into a gigantic, deep-throated green glass jug, which already weighs as much as a safe. I keep it right beside my bed, and it's no lie that I've still got that very first dime I ever made, buried somewhere under all those other coins. All silver, no pennies. How much exactly? Enough to get us through every tollbooth in North America should we decide someday to light out elsewhere.

Unlike the more down-to-earth married moms, ours harbors what I consider unrealistic expectations for both her kids and predicts that someday I'll become an investment banker. Possibly, although those few times she's hit me up for a loan for a carton of smokes or those worthless scratch tickets she occasionally brings home, I've turned her down flat for her own good.

In other words, we're a family. We stick together. We watch each other's backs, our twice-out-of-wedlock mom and her two bastard sons. But like I once said to Cole, so what? That whoever our fathers are, they're long done with us, and most days I wouldn't volunteer five minutes of my time if they did get in touch. Good riddance, I say, and when I tell Cole it's pointless to obsess and to beat himself up for what we never had, never knew, he says, "Speak for yourself, Glen. Know why? Because for me it's exactly the opposite." He says that he dreams, night after night, of an endless lineup of missing dads, their vacant stares voiding all claims to us, or to anyone. And scariest of all, he says, is that it's somehow our fault, a failure of our own making.

Our mom says, "That makes no sense." She says, "Please. For God's sake, Cole, it has nothing whatsoever to do with you two. How could it?" and I agree no percent.

"Okay, fine, but based on what?" is his ongoing inquiry, and she says, "Enough. No more of this. Ask me again when you're eighteen," and leaves it at that, like she's under some gag order. Of course we've done our share of nosing around in her closet and bureau drawers when she's at work. And Cole continues to eavesdrop whenever the phone rings or she dials out, but thus far nothing the least bit telltale. An old Kodak — there's that — but no snapshots or even a roll of undeveloped film in the camera.

Cole and I, we've shared our bedroom pretty much our entire lives, ancient army bunks and too little insulation in the ceiling, me on the bottom and Cole up top. I can't figure why he's up there since it's him who fights back the urge to cower and cry whenever a rainsquall or hail pelts down on the corrugated metal roof, covers thrown off, his face buried in the pillow, knees tight to his chest.

I've learned not to ask anymore if he's all right, or offer to swap places. If I did he'd go dead silent until the maelstrom quieted, and then get pissed and remind me that we're together due to fate and mysterious, uncontrollable forces in the universe, and *not* by choice. That there's an extra bedroom between ours and our mom's, and, "What, she falls asleep in one and wakes up in the other and you think that's normal?"

"It only happens when she drinks too much," I tell him. "That's all. That's how come she gets disoriented on her way back from the bathroom." And yet there *are* nights when I force myself to stay awake, and stare and stare down the tunnel of the hallway until my eyes adjust, and there she'll be, silently floating like a shadow through the dark, and the walls listing from side to side as she passes.

But by morning everything's always okay. She's up and around before we are. Her hair shiny and wet from the shower and the silverware washed and put away, and our crusty aluminum turkey or chicken-pot-pie containers already hanging outside for the cardinals and jays. She's resourceful that way. Says we ought to invest in half a dozen chickens or guineas, but I don't believe her, and my practical, responsible brain says, *Where's the coop for them to stay safe and to lay their eggs? And who, before the snow flies, is going to cleave the hatchet down and gut and pluck the damn things?* After all, we're not hippie, back-to-the-land types, Cole least of all. And so go ahead, try leading him to the chopping block and see how that plays out, this introverted, mixed-up kid who lives in constant fear of the ordinary, and lonely, and potentially violent day-to-day.

I mean, admit it, the reason he refuses to ever wear shorts goes all the way back to that summer our mom ordered us to sit on the front stairs while she slid a red-hot sewing needle through the engorged asses of deer ticks, our legs and ankles covered with them. They let go then, and the mouth holes they left, oval and raw, looked like infected mumps or measles, and burned like liquid fire when she swabbed them, not with rubbing alcohol, but instead with Listerine, which was all she could find in the medicine chest.

Even I had to bite down hard on my bottom lip and close my eyes, and Cole screaming bloody murder. Ever since, he hikes up these goofy, stretched-out white tube socks and refuses to cross any fields or ditches. Ask him to mow the back lawn and he'll go berserk, even if he *has* seen me do it barefoot a hundred or more times, the dull blade lopping the smoky heads off puffballs.

The school counselor says it's possible that he'll outgrow it, these phobias, but all I know is that the closer we get to Labor Day, the more he dreads the summer ending. Wants to reverse time before those bullies unleash their relentless back-to-school fury on him. Slapping his three-ring notebook from his hands and kicking it down the aisle, all the way to the rear of the bus, his stories and drawings torn and scattered under the seats. His four-color ink pen a disaster of clear plastic shards. When he tells me these horrors he envisions, he whispers.

"Maybe not," I tell him. "Could be those dopes won't do anything at all. Or ask Mom to drive you," but he glares at me, like I've just called him a twit or a pussy, a mama's boy. I say, "They so much as look sidelong at you . . ." but whatever I threaten or try to temper only sends him deeper into the demons. Back into our bedroom, where he climbs up onto his bunk, legs hanging down, and his body rocking forward and back while he speed-reads through dog-eared copies of *The Long Tomorrow* and *Journey to the Center of the Earth*. Reads them over and over, like the ending is the beginning and so he can never stop. I leave him be and turn on our worthless black-and-white TV in the living room and mute the sound in case he calls for me.

Most nights the screen is a blizzard of static by the time our mom finally gets home. She always checks first on Cole, and the reason I know something's different and wrong on this particular night is that she doesn't wake me by jingling my half of the coins up close to my ear. She says, "Glen, where is he? Where's Cole?" She's shaking my shoulder. She smells like cigarettes. It takes me all of five seconds to come wide-awake and leap right over the couch back and into our bedroom and check for myself. The window's open. There's a full moon, and I can see the silhouette of our mom's Bronco and hear the engine cooling and ticking down.

"Where is he?" she says again. "Where could he be at this hour? His bike's gone, too."

It takes mere minutes until we're busting toward the mine, the high beams cross-eyed like we're heading in opposite directions at the same time.

"Good God Almighty," she says, both hands gripping the steering wheel. "Whatever possessed you two? You're supposed to be watching out for him. Why would you go and do such a thing?"

Fieldwork. Research. The Twilight Zone. And I wish for the dashboard lights to begin pulsing, and the taped-up tailpipe to ignite in spectacular volleys of red-and-orange fire that rise and light up the treetops. For the radio to zap on and off at maximum volume, forcing her to pull over and cover her ears. Exactly like Cole does every other minute of every day that we're not up here, the guardians of what he calls the Kingdom.

"He'd never hurt himself, would he, Glen? Tell me that much at least. He'd never do that, correct?" and I say, "Promise me you won't unload on him. That first," and after she agrees, I tell her, "No. He'll be there. We're always careful and he'll know it's us by the sound of the car, but just in case let me be the one who walks up on him."

"All right," she says. "I'll stay in the car. I'll do that much but I can't guarantee for how long."

She's driving way too fast, gravel ricocheting like scattershot in the wheel wells. "Mom, slow down," I say. "Right ahead on the left's a two-track we want to take," and she brakes and hits her blinker, which hasn't worked in years. Then she checks the rearview, as if we're being followed. "Okay, better kill the headlights."

"Why?" she says, and slows to a crawl. "What's going on, Glen? Is this some plot against *me*? Have I done something wrong? Something terrible? Please, tell me right now if you think I have."

"I don't know," I say. "I don't think so."

"It's about your fathers, isn't it? It's always been about that," and I say, "Mine died in childbirth," but the tone's all wrong, the message. And before I can take it back she nods, and says, "Yes, in a manner of speaking. He did hold you, there's that, but for no more than a minute before he handed you back to me. I was eighteen. He'd just turned twenty-one. I closed my eyes, and when I opened them, he was nowhere to be seen. I never saw or heard from him again. Should I tell you more? Is this what you're after? The gory details?"

"No," I say, which is true and, unlike Cole, it always has been.

It takes another couple of minutes before the ground flattens out, goes bare and open, and the constellations pulsing everywhere outside the windshield.

I can't see into the basin, but there's the Big Dipper directly above. "Here's good. Park right here," I say, and she turns off the ignition, her window open. She's bare-armed to her elbows, no bracelets or rings, and already she's begun to shiver. I can hear it in her breathing, too.

"So this is it. The one place I asked you boys never to come. And look where we are. It's almost one o'clock in the morning. Go find your brother, Glen, and bring him back. God forbid that anything's happened to him." She says, "Damn you two. Why here? You'll be lucky if *your* kids are born with ten fingers and toes."

I don't say another thing. I get out and head straight for Cole's bike on its kickstand by the high ledge, the shoreline silver-haloed all the way around. I don't see him anywhere, the surface flat-calm, thick and clear, like crystal. The kind of night you can cup your hands around your mouth and imagine a single word echoing forever through the veins of flooded tunnels.

"Cole," I say, and it sounds more like a moan — my brother's name — and I say it again, over and over. "Cole, answer me," but he doesn't. At least not until I take off my shoes, my shirt, as if I've suddenly spotted his body rising from so deep down it might be nothing, a ghost, a mirage, pure panic setting in, and he shouts, "No, Glen, don't — I'm over here."

Like our mom, I'm chilled, too, and I think, *Yes, goddamn us all,* and I step back away from the ledge, and there he is, flailing his arms.

A non-swimmer with a diver's watch, sitting on the center seat of a permanently beached rowboat with no oars, and the northern lights reflecting heavenward and back, like dueling mirrors of endless ocean and sky.

To my knowledge he has never been held underwater. Never thrown from a dock, like I've heard some fathers do for fun. Those same fathers who take their sons fishing and camping, or attack with claw hammers the rotten backs of outhouses or sheds. Build tree houses and forts. Whistle for the dog—the tailgate down—to jump into the truck bed, a cold beer secured in the cup holder. Our mom has never so much as offered us a sip of whatever she's drinking. And, when she's consumed too much, she'll sometimes stare at us and, right out of the blue, say more likely than not we'll grow up to break some woman's heart.

It's as bright outside as daylight when Cole and I lift his bike into the back of the Bronco. Neither of us wants to ride up front with her, and so it's more like we're in a taxi. Except that she doesn't ask, "Where to?" or start a meter going. She pushes the lighter in, a ciga-rette between her lips. It seems like forever before it pops, and, when she takes that first deep drag, she could just as easily be waiting for someone to drive up and meet her, open the passenger-side door and slide in.

I've imagined it happening to me, Eileen Lickteig leaning her head against my shoulder, then straddling me as I stroke her hair. A dream still years off, and maybe that's why we're sitting like we are, arms crossed, elbows tucked, as far removed as humanly possible from one other. Whatever each of us is right this instant thinking would be way too angry or sad or flat-out crazy to say.

Our mom lowers the visor, as if half-blinded by the impossible brightness. Then she clears her throat like she's about to swing around and ream us out. Or maybe it *is*, finally, the right time and place to answer whatever questions we have about our dads. She's that furious, I can tell.

But she stays forward facing, the Bronco's idle rough, and the heater blasting away. She doesn't so much as glance in the rearview, like we're not even present. She shifts into drive, and U-turns back into that swirl of shadows and light as she maneuvers through the trees and out to the road. Stops. Looks both ways. "All set?" she says, more to herself than to us, and we go.

ON THIS DAY
YOU ARE
ALL YOUR AGES

AND THE LONGEVITY genes are on your side. Your mother, at eighty-one, still owns that same outdated two-bedroom, bath-and-a-half red brick ranch where you grew up, a valid driver's license, and a Buick Skylark that, as she says, was built to last.

And your father, former Special Forces, had *already* lived a dozen lifetimes before he died of unnatural causes. Not a shotgun or a noose or a hose attached to the exhaust pipe because nowhere in your family history is there any evidence of that. And even you, Marjorie Breit-weiser, a casualty of late-stage divorce and addiction to loneliness, will not be the first.

And most certainly not midmorning on a Saturday in April such as this—clear skies and the forecast going forward calling for temperatures in the upper sixties. If you could you'd bury the past and live each day as if it were your last. But the truth is you want her back, that feisty, quirky kid who, in recollection, keeps kissing her own wrist and calls it practice.

Remember that? The eleven-year-old who harangues against any elective surgery to correct those severely crossed and oversize eyes? It's a fact, especially when you're tired or upset, that they're apt to wander off on their own, and almost touch. But why tizz out about it is what you'd like to know. After all, your vision is twenty-twenty, and, as you insist, in the end that's all that really matters, isn't it? No floaters. No migraines or blackouts or seeing double. No dizziness or trances, and the world, as far as you can tell, in perfect focus. So what's the big hurry anyway? You're already wearing braces, and how many correctable features can there be in a single face? Besides, there must have been back then, maybe, and possibly even now someone out there somewhere determined to love you exactly as you are.

"Don't hold your breath," your mother says. It's no big deal, an upgrade, "A routine realignment is all," and you imagine two tiny, silvery blue wheels spinning silently behind your closed lids.

She reads you the riot act, calls you selfish, belligerent, and naïve. She says, "I don't need this." Says, "Snap out of it, Marjorie, before it's too late, or believe you me you'll forever regret this." She refers to you in moments of frustration as Miss High and Holy who can't see past your own stubbornness, a first-class drama queen.

Could be she's right, but screw the attitude adjustment. You like who you are, and when she holds up a hand mirror and says, "Honest to Christ," it's she who's rattled and shamefaced, not you. She still offers as evidence before and after photos of women and girls, and guarantees—100 percent—that the outcome will turn you gorgeous. Best in show, she jokes when she's in a better mood, as though you're some poodle or Shih Tzu or Pekingese. Talk about freaks of nature.

"Maybe," you say, but she says, "No, not if, when." She says, "Argument over. Now look at me," but your stare-downs of late have become so intense that sightlessness might seem a mercy.

AND THEN OUT OF NOWHERE it's 1977 and you've just turned fourteen. An only child of a single mother, and still a minor when Clifton Zelony unlatches and holds open the door to the toolshed behind his parents' house, as he will again and again over the next few weeks with bribes of cigarettes and ice-cold cans of his old man's Miller High Life.

He lives just down the street, around the corner, and it's impossible to determine anymore whether hormones or a simple case of the late summer doldrums brings you there. Either way there you are, a little tipsy. Beyond that? Well, he's not much to look at: gangly, a blond peach-fuzz mustache. Hardly ever smiles. Quiet for the most part, low-key, and, at least thus far, he appears harmless enough. Unlike the boys your mother repeatedly warns you about—those wild and wayward shaggy-headed creatures of excess needs and desires. The way-too-easy-to-fall-in-love-with heartbreak types, who, in the end, constitute nothing more than a giant waste of time and energy. She says, "Just remember to keep your damn legs crossed."

Which is less and less a problem, given that your interest in Clifton grows old in a hurry. The making out, the convoluted trails he charts across your body with his fingertips, then dinners down your tight, flat stomach with his tongue, the two of you curled up on the plywood floor among the rakes and spades and bulb planters, your breasts barely button knobs.

He's the first guy you've let touch you like this, and although he's unzipped your cut-offs and lifted the elastic of your underpants with his thumb, you haven't gone all the way. Nor will you—not yet and for sure not with him—and when you break it off a week before school begins he simply nods at first as if being ditched is just one more cruel and fucked-up initiation into adulthood. Except, of course, that he's gone tight-jawed and doesn't even blink. He leers, hate faced. As if from out of a mug shot, though that's still years away and since when is it a crime to sight down the length of one arm and squeeze an imaginary trigger?

"Ka-boom," he says. And sure enough he unleashes the cruelest litany of epithets and taunts you've so far endured: Inbred. Mongrel bitch. Lemur. Spider monkey. "A rescue mission," he says. A tease and a scag he wouldn't be caught dead with in public, though he hangs around to watch you put your T-shirt back on, and untangle an earring from your hair, which is long and dark and wavy. He's two years older, about to be a junior, but suddenly spooked silent when you look up and lock eyes, like you can see right through him into the godforsaken future of *both* your lives.

SOON AFTER ALL that, you do give in to the procedure. You say to your mother, "All right, I've changed my mind," and for a full week following you wear a blindfold, crisscrossing pirate patches. All day, all night, and you swear to Clementine Pugh, your gullible best friend and confidante, that rather than straightforward corrective surgery, the doctors went ahead and ordered two transplant pupils and corneas flown in nonstop from Brazil. Carefully packed in an urn of smoking dry ice. Like something better suited to a mausoleum shelf for safekeeping.

And no, you have *not* yet seen what you look like. Everything is pitch black, but on whatever day you finally do open your eyes, and turn on even the dimmest light, it will feel like fire, like touching a lit match to a tablespoon of magnesium. It will burn and burn, but for now in the shower you're like Helen Keller, your body braille, and the bar of almond-scented soap that washes over you holds images and secrets too terrible to ever disclose.

"Things *he* sees and dreams," you say. "Close up, in 3-D."

"Like what?" Clementine says, and you lean toward her and whisper that the deceased donor was a boy exactly your age. "Exactly *our* age," you say. "A dead boy's eyes," and she squints and backs away.

"I don't believe you," she says, but of course she does, and when you singsong, "One, Mississippi, two, Mississippi," she shakes her head and starts to cry. Glances this way and that before she flees into the ordinary, everyday visible world that has suddenly begun changing shape all around her.

When you actually do take off the patches what strikes you, from dawn to dusk, season after season, is that half a millennium is apt to elapse without notice. And that someone, perhaps Mr. DeWitt, your elderly next-door neighbor, is destined in the next half second to stop dead in his tracks and abandon his push mower on the uncut front lawn. He's already mowed and raked the entire backyard, bagged the cuttings, smiled over and waved to you like always. It's a day like any other: disappearing vapor trails overhead, and that ravenous and relentless shrill cawing of crows.

Except that going forward you don't see him anywhere for many days. Then a full month passes, and instead of the stairs, your mother explains in her matter-of-fact way that he's housebound now and rides a slow motorized lift to the second floor, and then back down. A walker, a wheelchair, a subscription to retirement radio, piped in from who knows where. He's suffered a stroke. His daughter is there to care for him, and, in anticipation of what comes next, she's added his name to the convalescent home's endless waiting list. A room thick with wintergreen and a view of either the road or the parking lot. *That* future or something like it, and no possible way by then to circle back and begin again.

"BUT *WE* CAN," you declare decades later, and you halfway imagine, in spite of your husband, Ward's, long, protracted response, a salvageable outcome. "Marjorie," he says. "For starters, how about we give it a rest, okay?"

The sun's not even up and because you've gone off again on that same tangent about how life begins at fifty he's already folded the morning paper and put it down beside his pancakes and scrambled eggs and bacon. He folds his arms and leans slowly back. It's pretty much the only exercise he gets anymore, this former college scholarship swimmer who railed and railed from the outset against ever having kids and confused good sex with doing the butterfly. If he'd had a better sense of humor, you'd have bought him a stopwatch by now, along with a free sample-pack of Viagra.

But it's been a while since any of that, the romps and moans and breathlessness, your hair in sweaty tangles. In fact, during the past few years you can count on one hand the number of times he's gotten into bed before you've drifted into deepest sleep, curled up on your left side, facing away, your diaphragm long ago stored in the bottom drawer of the nightstand, a relic from another era.

Still, you share certain interests. Politics, old black-and-white films, auctions and estate sales, the garden out back with its night-blooming flowers: raised beds of dragon fruit and evening primrose and Casablanca lilies. You've even taken a foreign-language class together in preparation for that promised and already twice postponed second honeymoon to Mexico, though even about this you rarely argue. You eat out every Tuesday and Saturday and, more often than not, converse in ways that make you feel present and necessary. For these reasons you've managed to remain optimistic and married for almost fifteen years and counting.

"I'm sorry," he finally says. "But why put off until tomorrow . . ." And once again it's Friday, but you can tell this Friday is unlike all the others, and you want more than anything in this life for him to take back what he's about to say. It's been coming, later than sooner as it turns out, but here it is, and by early evening he'll be packed and gone, a note on the kitchen table when you get home from the pharmacy, where you count capsules and pills and work the drive-thru window.

Prescription after prescription placed inside those thin white paper bags and stapled shut. Vicodin, Adapin, Zoloft, Lunesta. Methadone. Drops for earwigs, for cataracts, ointments for ringworm and canker sores, for boils the size of raw oysters. And worst of all, for those scars and fourth-degree body burns and skin grafts. You've seen the small children in profile, pale faces unlined and unblemished, flawless until they turn to see who's talking over the scratchy intercom to their mom or dad: that nosy woman asking for addresses, birthdates, verification of who they are. You can't help imagining their lives, what happened and how, the deep grief and remorse of such misfortune. Sometimes, when that hand reaches toward you with the clipboard and credit card for the co-pay, you almost toss the starched white smock you're wearing to the floor and walk out of there for good.

You've explained this to your husband, but there's a timetable, an ongoing countdown. As he points out, gone are the days of decent salaries and health benefits, any lasting loyalty to even the long-tenured like you. "And who, by the way, is hiring people our age?" he'd like to know. "So just hang in there, Marjorie. Hang on," and you do.

He's a CPA, a numbers guy, straitlaced, nose to the grindstone, a man born to balance the accounts of others. Orderly and measured and responsible. Kind. A good soul. And yet somehow, out of the blue, he works up the nerve to explain these last few years as the longest and most debilitating of his life. He calculates, on a scale of one to ten, a negative three, the days interchangeable and leading nowhere, except deeper into the dead zone of married life. And so why drag it out any longer? He's met a mum. He's in love and so there it is, out in the open. He says, "At last. Did you really not see this coming?"

"No," you tell him after maybe a full minute, as if his words have traveled an enormous distance to find you. You've intuited nothing, not a single slipup affirming even the slightest suspicion or disputed claim. Not a clue, and no matter how often or far you reverse the dots, you simply cannot connect them. Where you end up is where you always end up after thousands and thousands of hours on your feet, and the lunches you pack and unwrap so slowly that more than half your lifetime passes.

You put in for all the vacation days you've saved up, the leaves already red and gold, and the tight multicolored mum clusters glowing under the new moon. Along with the uncarved pumpkins on the front porch stairs, they help to dress up the emptiness of fall.

You stay busy by painting the ceilings, the interior walls of every room and hallway, and you remain indoors as if quarantined. Your husband has not come home, and won't. And, in advance of the divorce, you agree over the telephone to a fifty-fifty split of all assets. Right down the middle. Or, as he puts it, fifty cents on the dollar. Plus you get the house, with its new energy-efficient furnace and A/C, the driveway recently resealed, the mortgage paid down by half.

It's more than fair is what he argues, but at any cost he's the one flying high; you can hear it in his voice as clear as a cowbell. You might even in the ensuing months or years wish him well but definitely not yet. Forgiveness is a test against anger and loss; these take a while to get over, as it did with your father, a DOA at the ripe old age of twenty-nine.

That's your mother's story to tell. And she has, countless times, how he returned all screwed up to the Upper Midwest after back-to-back tours in those godforsaken jungles most people couldn't locate on a world map. Violent mood swings, and his only job offer was loading bull balls and hog cheeks and giant blood clots into idling semis at the rendering plant: part time, graveyard shift, and to which he'd finally said, "For fucksake," and went AWOL halfway through his fourth week.

Started pounding down what your mother called widow-makers. And cranked up the Beach Boys, and, in the predawn two thousand miles from the California coast, he caught a wave and for almost three full downtown blocks hung ten on the roof of a war buddy's speeding van in 1964. Like two barhopping frat-boy daredevils in fatigues and combat boots, when *he* should have been slow dancing in nervous circles around the hospital bed that night you were born. Five weeks premature: three pounds, eight ounces, and no wonder the truth comes to you again and again so long after the fact: that this, after all, is what men do.

LAST NIGHT another snowstorm and the schools are closed. The only gaff is that you're not a teacher, and with each sidesplitting shovelful you curse the delinquent plow guy to whom you've made clear what time you're expected, each and every weekday morning, to be at work. That's the thing, it's getting on toward nine thirty and the drugs in their plastic bins are waiting. Pills powerful enough to induce a coma, to slow down or speed up a heart.

It's minus fifteen degrees, and you're wearing an ankle-length goose-down parka, lightweight and black as a shroud. A scarf and a ski mask, too, your eyes bright blue in their dark sockets. You haven't even brushed your hair or put on any makeup, and because your mittens are already wet you shake them off and lift your half-frozen fingers to the oval mouth hole and breathe.

Every few seconds the wind kicks up, and you face away. Toward the picture window soaped last Halloween after you turned off all the lights and went to bed: *OGRE, WENCH, GHOUL.* But on this morning in midwinter disguise, you concede that the reflection staring back at you is none other than the grim reaper herself, your shovel a scythe, and that this first February, divorced and alone, has taken, minute by minute, a merciless toll.

You could lose your job, which you need more than ever. It wouldn't surprise you if the call came right now, as you stand hunched over, knee-deep, stock-still and shivering. You can hear the low-hanging power lines hum, and the thermostat is set at eighty-five just in case the electricity *does* go out. No fireplace or backup generator and the snow falling even harder, a total whiteout.

Like a dream, you think, and just like that it's All Hallows Eve 1972, and your mother, from as far back as you can remember, has designed and sewn every one of your costumes. As always, this one fits perfectly, like a second skin. This year you go as Joan of Arc, a young martyr your mother has read books to you about. And shown you reproductions of ancient paintings and fashioned you a helmet, and ballpeen-hammered an aluminum vest. A sword with an open-mouthed trick-or-treat sack dangling from the tip. You tap on the neighborhood doors with it, and grownups hand over the spoils: candy and coins, apples as round and shiny as blown-glass orbs.

"Who are you supposed to be, dear?" Mrs. McElvoy from down the street asks. She's old and wears one of those pointy bras under her sweater. Perfume so strong it makes your eyes sting.

"Guess," you say, and she says back, "Well, can you give me a few hints?" and you tell her, "Okay." You're a saint, nicknamed the Maid of Orleans, a protector of the French people during the Hundred Years' War, details you've memorized. The year is 1431.

Then you straighten your shoulders and say, like you're the lead in a school play, "Yet must I go and must I do this thing."

Mrs. McElvoy smiles and shrugs, her hair the color of smoke, and backlit by a hallway light so bright you imagine flames rising around *all* the magnificent, sacrificial witches throughout history who have been bound and burned alive at the stake.

NOW, AS ALWAYS, on those occasions when you visit your mother forty-five minutes away in Manistee, the last thing you do before you leave is lift and stare at the glassed, grainy black-and-white portrait of your father in that standup frame on the mantel. He's a handsome man, shiny black hair combed back, and the bones of his face a mirror image of yours. Two Purple Hearts. "A dead ringer," your mother says, but she always stops short of naming names anymore of film stars long deceased. She says instead, "If only he'd lost his trigger finger to a chipper or cherry bomb when he was a boy. Anything to have kept him home, for all the goddamn good his military service did for anyone."

She used to say, "Tell me, Marjorie, what sin did we commit to deserve this?"

"Nothing," you'd tell her, and she'd answer, "And for future reference, no. I'll never remarry," though you can't remember a single instance of ever having asked.

Today she goes silent after a verbal skirmish. She closes her eyes, and then, out of nowhere, asks, "When did you last hear from Parish?" Like *he's* your ex, and therefore grandkids must, in some unfathomable permutation, figure into the equation. She means Parish Mackey, a college sweetheart who, whenever he kisses you in memory or in dreams, still makes your nipples harden and ache.

Gordon Swogger, Billy Payne, Leo Shea—a roll call of the missing, men you've dated, one or two you might even have loved had they not stood you up in such hurtful ways. Your mother never forgets or confuses them, but you remember best by far Johnny Zale. It's 1989 and he's driven you home on spring break on his Harley, detouring almost two hundred miles northwest, from East Lansing on his trek farther north into the Upper Peninsula.

You're both road weary, chilled to the bone. Plus there's a hazy half moon, and the temperature falling, your one and only opening to invite him to spend the night, as he has a few times in your dorm room. There's little your mother can argue and not appear insensitive and rude.

He's met her before and so he says to you, "Thanks, but hey, three's a crowd, right? No worries. I've got some speed, I'm sure I can make it okay."

Maybe, but Marquette is still another six hours, not to mention those vast, low-lying stretches of dense fog along Route 2, and nothing but a broken, hypnotic yellow two-lane center line to follow.

And so you bring out clean sheets, a blanket and pillow. The two of you sit shoulder to shoulder on the pullout couch, talking even later into the night than usual. Your mother is asleep, her door closed. He touches the backs of your knees, your lips.

"Not here," you say. "Uh-uh." You say, "Sweet dreams" when he leans in yet again, and they are. But what you remember best after he sneaks into your bedroom and gently shakes you awake at first light to whisper, "I'm checking out, gotta go," is that shiny chrome chain snaked through his belt loops. And the billfold it attaches to in the back pocket of his jeans as he throttles away, bent over the handlebars, the ass cut out of his leather chaps, and the sky endless and silver-rimmed like a mirror.

"To hell and gone," you remember your mother said at breakfast. "All of them," meaning those wild and beautiful boys. "Let them go. Even if they plead on hands and knees, don't you ever give in and follow." How is it, you wonder, that she can remember them even now?

YOU CHANGE YOUR MAJOR last minute, from nursing to pharmacy. Three extra semesters to finally get your degree. But it fits you and you land a hugely better than expected job right out of college, which affords the freedom of your own place: a bare bones, reasonably priced, clean, and quiet efficiency in Traverse City. As well as your first car, a low-mileage Dodge Dart. In addition, you manage to pay back every loan ahead of schedule. And *still* you sock some savings away and promise yourself to someday travel both far and wide. New Zealand, maybe. Caracas or Acapulco in February or March. You like the sound of Swissair and imagine whispering to the pilot, "Doesn't matter. Wherever you're headed."

You grow used to your independence, to being alone, though friends worry, and Glenda from work comes up with an unasked-for prospect: "From all reports he's a nice guy. Good job, never been married. No red flags. Hey, it's worth a try."

"Another gift from the gods," you say, and she says, "Fine. But if you change your mind . . . " and the blind date who knocks that Friday evening on your front door arrives holding flowers, his khakis creased and pleated, spit-shined loafers, a monogrammed white Oxford shirt.

His name is Ward Beal and he takes you out half a dozen times before inviting you up to his place. Dinner, movies, sometimes a drink afterward. He's pushing forty. Just overweight enough that it doesn't surprise you when he forgoes the stairs and waits for the freight elevator door to open. An empty, humid, dark, and airless square box of a space, like something a small missile might rocket out of. It's fusty smelling and claustrophobic, *and What*, you ask yourself, *was I think-*

ing? But only until the elevator stops and you step out into a century-old studio apartment above a bookstore on the town's main street. Paintings and track lighting, exposed brick walls, and floor-to-ceiling windows with a distant view of the bay—the place, immaculate.

Ward never raises his voice or cuts you off midsentence, and apologizes profusely the one time he bears down so hard on a letter he's drafting to the editor about traffic and the lack of parking that the pencil lead explodes in a thousand different directions. "He's passionate," you tell Glenda. "And smart, too," but leave out that he's still a work in progress when it comes to the bedroom.

"There's no option in the rental agreement to renew the lease," Ward says, and you see it as an omen. The timing feels right for the two of you to make a commitment. You keep it simple, and elope on foot a few blocks south to the justice of the peace. And sign papers later that afternoon on a newly constructed split-level on a cul-de-sac with asphalt so smooth and black it looks at night like a deep, slow bend in a river you can float down forever.

YOU'VE BEEN ORPHANED five weeks in ICU, and now, whenever you cry, your mother is there to lift you out of your crib. It's not advised and yet she carries you from room to room, nursing you through these first nights home with song. The motion is dirge-like, minor key, and frightens you so much you learn to stay quiet, to lie still. The crib is not in her bedroom, but the walls are thin and you can hear her ragged breathing, the way she suppresses and chokes down the air.

But listen to this: in the daylight she hums. She inserts the pacifier into your mouth and bends even lower and whispers, "Hi, Marjorie," and carefully opens your eyes even wider with her index fingers and thumbs. You watch her pupils dilate into two perfectly synchronized gold dots. You follow them wherever she looks: out the windows, at the TV with the sound turned off, at those government checks that arrive each month, and her childlike scribble that endorses them.

Other times she stares transfixed at nothing, her eyes blank, glazed over, and she whispers to herself in tongues. Or plays solitaire at the kitchen table, where you sit strapped into a baby carrier, the kings and jacks the same bright red as her lips and nails.

Your favorite game is hide-and-peek, the way her fingers splay and then her hidden face appears like a vision. Furthermore, that's also when she confers with you: "Are you a happy girl?" she says, a dozen times over just to be certain. But she worries, too, and when she hunts up the different doctors' telephone numbers, you send silent signals pleading, "No, no, no."

She pencils in every appointment, and with a Magic Marker crosses each day off the calendar with a fat black X. You like the smell, like the cool scent of rubbing alcohol, and the way her fingertips play different tunes on your belly and back.

If the stroller tires were cast in brass, they'd carve deep grooves in that quarter-mile square of sidewalk that surrounds your block—a couples-only-with-kids kind of block, though you don't see the fathers often, and your face pinches at the sound of their coarse, open-throated voices. Sometimes they call your mother's name, but it's a furious, concentrated gait she maintains until you're out of earshot. That's when she slows down and you watch the illuminated undersides of the clouds as they ferry giant pools of sunlight across the endless sky. It's this pace you like, and how you can magically hold your own bottle with your own two hands now.

Your mother's thin, back in shape already, and sleepless some nights she carries you outside, wrapped in a blanket. She stands in the center of the small fenced-in backyard. "Look, Marjorie," she says, and you point, too, at the Weaving Sister, the Polish Bull, the Outer Kitchen. "The Wreath of Flowers," she says. "And there's the She-Goat, the Sea Stone, the Calf of the Lion."

Later in the summer comes the aurora borealis, those meteor streams that glitter and disappear in showers of pink and gold. Even after they vanish the grass is speckled silver. And the dark interior of the house also brightens, and you can see into your bedroom to the mobile that orbits back and forth like a mirage in the air currents above your crib

She lowers you, barefoot, to the ground. You wobble on your fat knees—you of the future slim waist and dancer's legs. Your mother, backing away, gets down on *her* knees, arms outstretched, and says, "Okay. Come to me, Marjorie."

You do not cry or sit down. You open your clenched fists and take that first impossible bowlegged step on your way to her. The distance covers approximately seven feet. It's easier than you imagine, moving like this through the shadows cast by that same moon, almost full again and rising.

THAT
STORY

WHEREVER MY MOM FINDS these articles I haven't a clue. All I know is that she clips them out and hands them to me to read. "Look, Fritzi, another miracle," she says, the most recent having occurred somewhere outside San Francisco.

For a good laugh I pass them along to Dieter and Brinks while we smoke in my dad's Plymouth Fury, the odometer frozen at 172,605 miles. The car is up on blocks, transmission shot and hubs painted purple. Rear risers but no tires, and snow up to both doors so we have to crawl inside, like it's an igloo or a fort, and always with some half-wrapped notion of someday firing it alive and driving hell-bent away from Bethlehem. Not the one in Pennsylvania, but a town so remote you can't even locate its position on a USGS map.

And therein resides both the irony and the farthest far-flung implausibility that somebody hereabouts discovers a visage of Christ in a lint screen at the local Laundromat, and that then, along with our name, we got ourselves a shrine and a destination to boot. "Imagine it," my mom says, but the idea of a million pilgrims desperate to put a knee down in this nothing town suddenly adjacent to God and heaven confounds even the dreamer in me. And yet, as misguided as such an influx sounds, it's what she's apparently banking on. Which might explain why she's hand-painting all those Baby Jesus Christmas ornaments, preparing to make a fortune off the endless caravans of sinners soon to arrive here in the provinces. But she says, "Nope. Uh-uh." They're nothing more than another scheme designed to fill and quiet time. Besides, she says, each month at the diner she always manages to sell at least a few to the truckers to take home to their wives.

I hate to admit it, but a miracle is precisely what it'll take to hire a lawyer high profile enough to enter an appeal and get my dad's sentence overturned from first-degree manslaughter to self-defense. Guilty or not, my mom maintains, when a married man slurps bar vodka from some strange woman's navel, he's going to pay a heavy price somewhere along the line. I remember how, right after the trial, she sat me down at the kitchen table and held both my hands and said, "Fritzi, listen to me. All premature deaths are wrongful deaths. But some, like this one, they're so senseless it makes them more wrong than the others. It makes them," she said, "eternally unforgivable."

Their divorce, final come May, has for a long while now been inevitable and therefore okay, I guess. Except for Bobby Bigalow, my mom's new boyfriend. Every word that falls from his loud mouth is either a rule or a sermon, and whenever he mentions my dad I can feel him present in my balled-up right fist. I know all too well that a single punch placed perfectly to the temple can kill a man, and so I afford Bobby Bigalow a wide berth. I'm only five-foot-six, but place a bet that I can't hoist a frozen hay bale over my head and you'll lose. Not that I'm prone to feats of strength or violence, but if he ever touches me or mistreats my mom, I swear I'll take that first swing and at least rearrange his dentistry, that sneer of a smile, those tight snake lips. Maybe send him packing with a jaw wired shut and eating through a straw—though of course there's my mom to contend with, and thus the quandary.

Dieter and Brinks and me can't see him, but we know he's standing not ten yards in front of us, eyeballs straining, and so in unison we drag all the harder on our Lucky Strikes, imagining ourselves magnified behind the windshield. Tough guys you come at with a length of pipe and who leave teeth marks in the metal.

A fit father or not, my dad taught me to never take one backward step, no matter what, and for starters there's that tradition to honor and uphold. Besides, I've never been fingerprinted or booked on even a single juvenile misdemeanor charge.

Flat-out lucky is Bobby Bigalow's take, and I'd second that—but never face-to-face the way he'd like. He's the type, you confess anything and he dangles it in front of you like a noose. What he wants is for me to shape up, to shit-ditch what he refers to as my "attitude and lack of focus," and commit to a new start before it's too late. Beginning with my friends, "those ones," as he calls them. He means tribal kids. (I'm one-quarter Ottawa on my dad's side, my hair shiny blue-black just like his. The resemblance in our facial features, however, is not all that close except in the eyes—"like night minus the moon," as my mom in happier days used to proclaim.) We've grown up together, all three blood brothers, and when Dieter's snowmobile is up and running we like to shoot the glass insulators from the tops of the telephone poles with our pellet rifles. Or ding the silver dining cars mere inches below those lighted windows where couples leaning forward keep toasting their lives, the train whistle within minutes fading into the invisible distance.

Right now, we blow slow-motion smoke rings above the head of the DayGlo dashboard Saint Christopher, perpetually open-fingered and palms up, who seems to say, "Okay, fine. But you're fifteen years old, for Chrissake, and so just what, pray tell, is the goddamn battle plan going forward?"

It's late February and the ashtray is packed with a fat stack of Trojans, like it's a free, customized in-car dispenser. We've got a bottle of Thunderbird, which Dieter scored on the reservation. Like my dad I've got no alcohol tolerance, so just a few quick hits and I envision a fig bush flowering inside Gloria Masterson's skintight Levi's. She's never afforded me the time of day, but there's a buffalo robe on the backseat just in case, and even the thought of it warming those impossible contours of her body accelerates my heart rate by plenty.

I can see my mom peeking out through the living room window, her hands cupped to her face like blinders. Everybody staring at everybody else, and no one advancing or uttering a single sound. A virtual standoff. Our prefab is a repo, two bedrooms and the wall so thin between them that some nights I can hear the static of my mom's nylon stockings as she undresses for bed after a double shift at the Honcho out on old Route 668, just north of the four-way stop. Out on the void, as she says, where idling, slat-sided transport trailers shake the entire parking lot like some low-grade version of the San Andreas Fault. I've seen it firsthand, the plates and silverware rattling on the Formica tables and countertops. My mom gets long hours and low pay, but jobs are tough to come by, and because we're barely hanging on she's locked in there against her long-term wishes. She's first on the seniority list, and I can't recollect when she last called in sick. Or when her credit card wasn't maxed to the hilt.

In one of the articles she gave me, a waterspout somewhere in South America spewed up coins of solid silver and gold. Not a thing you'd think to hope or wait around for, but there it is to consider, as opposed to the cash register that she tends day after day, all sticky with pitted nickels and dimes and quarters. Her dream is to someday see the Himalayas, though she's never even one time in her entire life left the state. Mark my words: Bobby Bigalow is not her ticket to anywhere you'd read about in a guidebook or travel brochure.

He's from Texas, an ex-rodeo cowboy out of Amarillo—or so he claims. He's got a slightly stooped back, so I calculate it's possible some pissed-off Brahman bull whiplashed him into early retirement a few lifetimes ago. Dieter's verdict is pisswilly on that, and Brinks agrees: Bobby Bigalow's just a self-glorified blowhard. He's got hair like General George A. Custer, wavy and blond, and I don't blame my mom for wanting company, but when the metal storm door opens and he steps back inside, I say, "Fuck him."

"And the horse he rode in on," Brinks says, though it's a Chevy Silverado he drives, and sometimes he'll rev it up real loud before he leaves, glasspacks growling, always the near side of midnight. Always after a few beers on the couch with my mom, arm around her neck or waist, and as she closes the blinds now I can see the vibrating blue waves cast by our secondhand, wide-screen Sony Trinitron.

At least for the time being the arrangement isn't live-in, and so I suppress any impulse to tell my dad about what's transpired on the courtship front. I will, however, as a last resort if at some point I need his counsel. On the final Sunday of every other month is when we talk, at 7:00 p.m. sharp. And it's only because he inquires that I betray my mom's whereabouts. Battalion II bingo, I tell him. Same exact routine replayed in every single solitary conversation. "Yes, she drives herself," I say, but what I withhold is that it's also where Bobby Bigalow calls out the numbers that have sent my mom home a winner these last few times in a row. It's where they met. An omen, she says, that against all odds she and I are fated for a life of lesser burdens.

During those allotted fifteen contact minutes, my dad says her name—Laila—a lot, in ways that turn each next sentence lonelier than the last. He's never denied that trouble feeds the passions of bad men, and on the witness stand he said simply, in his own defense, that he did not, first off, consider himself to be among them, leastwise not by intention. Just some nobody, he said, with a pint in the glove box and a drinker's lack of judgment—and, no, he conceded, he was not ignorant of a record of arrests too long to overlook after a Sunday night bar fight turned deadly.

"Then you're spared now to contemplate a different life going forward," the judge said. "But for the one you've mangled thus far, Mr. Boyd, you've exceeded your quota of last chances. For which I hereby sentence you to eighteen years in a maximum-security prison without the possibility of parole." Bars and razor wire and turrets and armed guards—that's how my dad describes the joint. "The big hole," he calls it. He says piss in the chili long enough and right here's where you end up, all dulled out and dead to the entire world.

"Bum rap," Brinks says. "I ask you, where's the justice?" He means that another weekend's shot, and we're out of cigarettes, the smoke so thick inside the car that I crack the window. There's a ladder that leans against the house, and a path I keep shoveled up to the roof peak for when the motor on the rotating TV antenna seizes. Mostly all it takes is half a dozen cupped breaths and a single knuckle rap to get it started again, but I refuse to watch the tube in Bobby Bigalow's presence. Dieter, as if he's reading my mind, says, "Well, you want this waste out of the picture or what?"

The honest answer's as dumb as trying to stare down the sun. The night air is frigid and still, and as my dad sober used to say, a man's mind in winter isn't meant to be enlightened, or sought after, and any attempt then at decision-making only invites grim and sorry thinking. I'm eye level with the snowdrifts that the wind has sculpted, the temperature's single digit at best, and it's beyond me why I say what I say, but I do, inviting trouble of a magnitude that we don't need and yet sometimes covet. I say, "Yeah, big-time," both hands locked on the Fury's steering wheel, and envision running Bobby Bigalow off the road and deep into the frozen turnip fields stretching away in all directions.

"It'd at least break the boredom," Dieter says. "There's that." He's got a deep voice and braids that sway when he walks, and every single paper he writes for English class is about the vanished nations rising up again. At school we stick close together, and if anyone wisecracks about the amulets he wears, we're a small war party to deal with. The same goes for Bobby Bigalow, who's a grown-up version of that same small-minded, small-town bully. He potshots us and takes cover behind my mom's loneliness, never smiling or offering to drive Brinks and Dieter home so they don't have to snowshoe those five miles each way just to sit in a backyard beater in the bitter cold.

"Why would anyone in his right mind do that?" Bobby Bigalow asked a few weeks back, and in my best attempt at a nasally Texas drawl, I said, "'Cause we ain't got a rowboat. That's why."

"Ha, ha, ha," he said. "Talk that bullshit and you and me, pal, we real plain and simple got us a problem to reconcile."

He leaned so close to me then that I could see the pockmarks on both his cheeks flare crimson. A grown man's glare I'd never seen fastened on a kid before, but I thought, *Hate-stare somebody else, you Lone Star loser.* The only scare tactic that had ever worked on me was when my mom threatened to leave. And sometimes she did go off for a day or two, with my dad stammering in her absence, "Honest to God, Fritz. Honest to God," like it was a double vow to fix everything that had, for years, spun further and further out of control. Speeding tickets and DWIs and racking up points enough to have his license revoked ten times over. Resisting arrest, disorderly conduct, urges that over the long haul define, as my mom insists, a weak man's feverish nature.

Brinks says, "The Quonsets. Let's blindfold him and escort him there."

That's where the turnips are temporarily stored after harvest, on dirt floors cut deep like bunkers. No windows, and even in summer it's always cool, the perfect place to build our ritual fires. Shavings and sticks and just enough flame to get our knife tips glowing. Check out our inner arms and you'll witness remnants of an ancient art, the raised scars long and blade-thin and climbing almost up to our elbows.

Bobby Bigalow's got matching spur tattoos on his biceps and a silver belt buckle big as a shield. And those gaudy western shirts with fake pearl cuff and button snaps. He's a sorry-looking stand-in for anyone I might consider habitable company for my mom. She's thirty-eight, strawberry-blond and narrow-hipped, and still pretty enough for men to get the fidgets when she walks by. So, sweet-talking Bobby Bigalow into relocating somewhere else won't be an easy sell. He's already acting like a stay-around, helping himself to beers and snacks from the fridge, and sometimes shuffling the mail as if searching for something that's his.

He complains that if he doesn't time it perfectly, he gets caught at the crossing gate, warning lights and bells and those freight cars throwing up sparks, and I'm halfway thinking right there's our optimum ambush spot: on the far side of the rails, so that after the sleepers and the caboose get past, there we'd be, the single high beam of our snowmobile bearing down like a phantom train about to pancake his sorry ass.

Dieter's waiting on parts so he can rebuild the carburetor in auto shop. He figures by midweek. But for right now, before he and Brinks trek home, he mimics the man in Spokane whose reattached left arm at nightfall points involuntarily at the Northern Cross, according to one of my mom's articles. Not that we buy any of it, that's for sure, but it nonetheless provides us some hilarity. Holy Mary, Mother of God, you lose a limb and sew it back on and all you can think to do out there under the heavens each night is reach up and thank your lucky stars?

Brinks says, "Man, if it's me I hit the casino and honk down on the lever of a thousand-dollar slot and watch the place light up like a munitions factory."

Dieter's all over that and I am, too. A little revenge for the years our dads lost to the gambling and the booze, for those declarations to change everything that ever hurt or harmed us if only they could. One summer, our faces streaked with war paint, we sent up smoke signals to the gods on our dads' behalf. If certain girls happened by, we'd turn to them and tom-tom the drums of our flat, naked stomachs, hoping they'd stop and maybe dance for us.

That failed to happen, then or ever, and here we are, me and Dieter and Brinks. When we bother to attend, we each maintain a steady C-minus average in a much-lower-than-average school district so far north that the cloud light hovering some nights turns the landscape a bluish-gray shade that's either gorgeous or violent, depending on your state of mind. Ours hasn't been that great of late, and to make matters worse my mom appears more and more dazed by bogus notions about Bobby Bigalow.

"He lies," I tell her. "He's a bully and a sneak." But her standard comeback is that he treats her well and that I shouldn't begrudge her another chance with a man.

"Those flank steaks," she said. "He's the one who bought them, not me. Please, don't judge him so harshly, Fritzi, inasmuch as you can't possibly know in advance how a thing might turn out in the end."

I figured she'd interject my dad as a negative example, but she didn't. Which in its own cruel way made him appear even more expendable in our lives going forward. It's as if Bobby Bigalow's got her under some spell. I've seen her turning this way and that in front of the full-length mirror, her hair down, wearing nothing but red lipstick and a slip, and making silent-still music with her hands on her hips.

Dieter says that you can crush dry gumroot and swamp irises into a fine yellowish-blue powder and boil it into a tea that forces the fork-tongued to speak the truth or else their skin puses up and peels away. But he can't recall the exact mixture or the other herbs, and the tribe's last medicine man died long before we came into this life. And any how, if we wait for late spring all might be forsaken.

"We'll figure something," Brinks says as he crawls out the window, and half a dozen snowshoe lengths later he and Dieter are out of sight. They come and go in silence, leaving no tracks or drag marks, because a few weeks back we attached a horsehair tail to the ass end of the snowmobile. The two five-tined pike spears we carry with us are spoils from a raid over on Lake Tonawanda, where we war-whooped and circled the shanties to make certain nobody was inside when we finally kicked open the door of one of them. Nobody other than those nude centerfold pinups, of course, tacked to the wall and staring back at us, with their slightly parted lips all glossy and blistered in the blue flames of my dad's brush-chromed Zippo and Brinks and Dieter's pilfered Bics. And so go ahead and try following them across the stark, windswept pastures and fields of white moose and deer and coyote, and just see how long before you're completely turned around out there where the spirit world is everywhere alive.

HERE'S MY MOM'S BEST ONE YET: a capstone gets jimmied from a long-abandoned well in the Ozarks and blind lungfish cry out in the voices of angels.

"Poetic," Dieter said.

"Downright inspiring," Brinks chimed in, all crocodile with a case of the weepies. Wet-vac all the way and, right, real funny, but maybe all miracles are a matter of need and deceit—all honest Injun horse-shit, as Bobby Bigalow says about Dieter and Brinks, and sometimes about me, though never when my mom's within earshot. I've seen him fingering her Christmas ornaments and eye rolling and shaking his head. I've seen him drink milk straight from the carton and then stare at those missing children in a way that blames everyone but himself, my mom's personal savior. And mine as well, if only I'd offer up some measure of contrition and a commitment to believing in forces other than myself and my two pull-trap friends. Yeah, we've got a few illegal beaver and muskrat sets, but so what? Not that Bobby Biga-low'd know a thing about where they're at. If he did he'd turn us in first thing to Church Stoner, the CO who's been itching to bust us for years, but even he—who's grown up in these parts—can't track us.

But a week or so after that night in the Fury we tracked Bobby Biga-low, and it's possible that he and my mom went dancing like she said this past Friday night, but Dieter hit seventy-five miles per hour on the snowmobile to position us at our outpost on Summit Hill. We could see the lights of town. The crisscrossing of the streets, the dull red pulse of the Grand Union sign, and Bobby Bigalow hooking a right toward that strip of drive-ins and cut-rate, off-season motels. Which merely reinforced that nothing is sacred or safe with him around. I suppose I could have waited up to interrogate my mom, but to what end other than to start my own blood throbbing? And I backed off on the attack front anyway, so as not to arouse or inflame suspicion.

Until this morning when, before boarding the school bus, I said, "It's my house, too," and she did not say back, "Of course it is," or, "It always will be," like I'd anticipated. She said, "Yes, within reason," but anyone reasons this out and they've identified the source of all our impending anguish and grief. She doesn't see it and no doubt won't if I don't intervene on her behalf.

"It's not an open subject, Fritzi, and I'm tired of feeling so disenchanted and god-awful all the time. I've been too long at my wit's end, but I'm dating someone now, and it's not as if they've arrived in twos and threes. Have they? I know how resentful you are, but I don't want us to face off like this all the time. And whatever happens going forward, I want you to promise not to hold it against me."

I remained silent and stone-faced. We both did, and then she said a thing I knew might someday prove to be accurate, though to hear it spoken conjured in me a consideration I hadn't until that moment ever fathomed, and hoped I'd never in a different situation have to again. She said, "If you want to blame someone, blame your father. And if he asks, you tell him the truth. That he, and he alone, is the one who led us to where we find ourselves on this very day. As crazy convoluted as it sounds, he's the one who introduced us to Bobby. Tell him that, Fritzi. And tell him that except for a man being dead, I'm glad in the end that he did."

Dieter met me as I stepped off the bus, and said, "Everything's still a go?" and I said back, "Full bore," and we both nodded. We've stashed two sickles and a roll of electrician's tape in the Fury, and the wolf headdress that he signed out from the tribe for next week's history class show-and-tell, plus a peace pipe that we've been sucking without success for residual effects.

The forecast is for a blow out of Canada. A foot or more of snow, and you watch—that'll be Bobby Bigalow's ruse to finally spend the night. And I don't mean on the couch, and I don't care to wake to that next morning, and breakfast, and the final rubble of my dad's last possessions boxed and banished to Goodwill without me even getting to go through them.

I ditched early, right after civics class, and by late morning I'd already stopped obsessing about what our civics teacher, Mr. DeSclafani, called a God-spot, this bay in the brain that functioned to dial back the onset of anger and treachery and revenge. I didn't raise my hand, but if I had I would have mentioned the afghan that Bobby Bigalow unfolds and drapes around my mom's shoulders just to tick me off. And how sometimes he even winks at me from right there behind the couch. In my head I hear my dad's old rant: "Give ground one time to that, and you'll be doing it on a daily basis." And so it only makes sense to "bring 'em on, all comers. Every last Fo, Fuck, and Fum."

And tonight as Dieter and Brinks and I see it, we're going to right some wrongs is all. If things foul up maybe we'll move on Dieter's backup plan to screw a spigot into one of those giant wine casks we've seen stacked on the boxcars and drink our way west on the rails to the Columbia River Gorge. Out where his dad lived for a short while after a stint in the service. And where he fished for king salmon that danced on their silver tails in the froth and the sunshine, right there below what he called the great nonstop booming of the falls. Last we heard he was living outside Montreal, and I suppose someday that might be a destination for us, too. I can't legally visit my dad until I turn eighteen, but like Dieter says, at least there's no guesswork concerning his whereabouts.

My mom's scheduled to work a double shift, and she left wearing a polished, silver-veined quartz stone around her neck. I've never seen it before. A gift from Bobby Bigalow no doubt, who just last night complained about the lousy water pressure like somehow he owns that right. The pipes not being buried deep enough under the frost line's the problem, and so we have to let the faucet slow-drip whenever the mercury dips below fifteen degrees. Sometimes I'll place an empty, upside-down ice-cube tray directly under the tap in the kitchen sink just to drive him batshit. I spare him not one reminder that in my eyes he and my mom are maybe hot-wired for the short run but are destined for an abrupt chill down.

He's clueless that Dieter and Brinks tracked him home to some double-wide off Tapico. Off Arrowhead. Off a no-name two-track that backs up to state land where the proposed hydraulic dumpster was supposed to go. All that's there is a giant hole half filled with the dead weight of ruptured appliances and bedsprings and bald tires. TVs with bullet holes through the picture tubes. Plus a few metal shopping carts that we hauled out for the caster wheels we used to build ourselves three suicide skateboards.

We've remapped our attack-and-capture strategy in favor of just happening to be in Bobby Bigalow's neck of the woods later tonight. You know, to search the clearings and snow fields for a high-stepper who might teach us how to make our squaws go dumb between the bedsheets—a phrase he let slip that caused the first time I'd seen my mom flinch in his presence, her mouth muscles going taut. I wanted to say, "There. That's who he is outright. A croaker always running his lily livered mouth, and why parlay the likes of him into heartbreak? Why him?" But they're a twosome, plain and simple. And, like Brinks says, all love's a fluke either temporary or lifelong, and without incentive Bobby Bigalow ain't about to scare or bugger off anytime in our immediate future.

But as I wait for Dieter and Brinks to pick me up, I'm all Indian, and the sickles are razor sharp and already taped to the insides of my wrists for a better grip. Like curved tomahawks or talons. And the wolf's skull plate a perfect fit, my face smeared with lampblack from the inside glass of the kerosene lantern my dad always used whenever we dipped smelt in Otter Creek.

There's a full moon and the air's frostbite cold, and I remember how my dad said years ago, when I inquired, that he'd proposed to my mom under a meteor shower, the tracer tails so intense they turned the skyways platinum. There's Orion, the hunter. And this is the car in which my parents first dated, first kissed, and only since Bobby Bigalow does my mom, without a second's hesitation or any apparent regret, say straight-faced that it was all a colossal mistake, "a marriage so doomed and misguided." Think on that awhile like I do: I pull up short of calling her a liar, but she's nonetheless knocking a lot of careless and hurtful wrong words about.

That's a fact, and rather than let her pawn her wedding ring, last month I zinged it with my slingshot as far into the constellations as I could. And is that not, when I hear the muted roostertailing of Dieter's snowmobile up a certain draw still half a mile distant, why I roll down the car window and crawl outside without a second thought? Yes, on all fours, dressed in furs and wolf fangs and ready, finally, to move out across the frozen tundra, under the miracle of these winter stars.

"NO MERCY," Brinks says. He's holding a ball-and-claw table leg, and Dieter's brandishing one of the pike spears. There's no barking dog to quiet, but there is a second vehicle in Bobby's driveway. It's definitely not my mom's Cherokee, and it's parked directly in front of the pickup, which appears to be sniffing the Jeep's hind end like it's got in mind to hump it.

We're standing back a short ways from the slider. No blinds and the kitchen lit up, but nobody's stepped into view yet. I've never seen wallpaper like this before. A jungle clot of jonquils — all summery and yellow — and flocked here and there amid them are a few oversize roses the dark-blood color of mulberries.

"Some weird shit here," Dieter whispers, and it's true that the icicles hanging halfway down in front of the glass distort this woman who appears out of nowhere like a ghost among the vines and tangles. She's stark naked, and she stops at the stove and leans over and turns her head sideways to light a cigarette from one of the front burners. Then she leans against the counter and folds her arms over her breasts like she's shy or cold, or maybe even afraid and cowering.

No one says so, but we despise Bobby Bigalow all the more when he swaggers in zipping up his pants. What I notice most, though, is the ceiling, textured and flecked like ours with fake chips of mica.

And how this woman is knock-kneed and shivering as the moon disappears and more snow starts to fall. It's the exact same posture I've seen my mom assume too many times—though bundled up of course. I imagine all four gas jets open full, and the oven turned on the way we always have it to survive the night whenever our furnace conks.

"It ain't his place," Brinks says. "He don't live here, Fritz. It's hers, and now how the fuck may I direct your call?"

The only one I'm certain owns a cell phone among us is Bobby Bigalow—some new fancy-ass gadget that takes snapshots and that he keeps holstered on his hip. I've heard it ring, though never have I seen him use or answer it. What I flash on instead is one of those old-fashioned cameras, a bellows and a black hood and that slow, hand-held explosion of gunpowdery light. This would make a one-in-a million portrait, a classic: three armed and angry young chieftains standing side by side, the single threat of each of us tripled in the camera's eye.

"Let's dial this up or duck out of here," Dieter says, ice forming on the black buzzard and eagle feathers in his hair.

"Your call," Brinks says. "Either way." But when he passes me the wineskin it's my dad I imagine, half-drunk and fury-fisted and cleaving through the snow toward whatever door that Bobby Bigalow is about to exit.

Like father, like son, and it takes only a matter of seconds for me to calculate that weeks or months or years from now I might own up that "Here, overtaken by rage and revenge, is where I pummeled and perhaps maimed or even killed a man." Or, "Here's where I stood with my only two friends on earth one February night. The snow suddenly coming down so hard that a man my mom believed mattered passed unaware within ten feet of us after being with another woman. We could smell her perfume, her nakedness, his beery breath, could hear him hiss between his teeth as we watched him disappear."

Neither is a confession whose details can redeem a thing. But have I mentioned the jukebox at the Honcho? Merle Haggard and Mickey

Gilley, and truckers who change dollar bills into quarters, and my mom who's destined to start humming those heart-drain tunes again real soon, one way or another, no matter what goes down here.

When I give the word we sneak away. Dieter starts the snowmobile. "Hang tight," he says, and it's as if nothing can touch us as we tear-ass into all that whiteness, flying blind and the trees coming at us out of nowhere. There's an abandoned cellar hole we somehow avoid, and then we're airborne over the not-so-high rock-face outcropping we've survived at least a hundred times. The snow's coming in waves like wings, and we rise, I swear it. Three lost-cause kids in crazy getups, straddling not the wide seat of a Polaris sled, but rather a bareback horse, its black tail combed shiny by the wind.

That story. The one riddled with God-spots and paybacks and love full-blown for women we might someday make giddy and, despite our best intentions, betray. Thunderbird and muscatel. Dads who've gone missing, and a mom who, against all the evidence, believes in miracles she's determined to pass along to her son.

ABOUT
THE AUTHOR

Jack Driscoll is a two-time NEA Creative Writing Fellowship recipient and the author of eleven books, including the short story collections *Wanting Only to Be Heard*, winner of the AWP Short Fiction Award, and *The World of a Few Minutes Ago* (Wayne State University Press, 2012), winner of the Society of Midland Authors Award and the Michigan Notable Book award. His stories have appeared widely in journals including *The Georgia Review, The Southern Review, Ploughshares, Missouri Review, Michigan Quarterly Review,* the *Pushcart Prize Anthology,* and *New Stories from the Midwest.* He currently teaches in Pacific University's low-residency MFA program in Oregon.